Praise for Lena Matthews'
Joker's Wild: Stripped Bare

"Reviews: Kudos' for Lena Matthews! This story was wonderful .... I highly recommend having a cold drink handy since this story is very steamy."

~ *Valerie Eisiminger, Rites of Romance Reviews*

"Be prepared to break out the ice cubes as STRIPPED BARE is one smoking hot tale. If you enjoy your romances sizzling, then you won't go wrong here."

~ *Holly Tibbs, Romance Reviews Today*

Recommend Read "Jokers Wild: Stripped Bare is an amazing book! Brody and Melissa are unforgettable characters that you will hate to say goodbye to."

~ *Tewanda, Fallen Angel Reviews*

Stripped Bare is humorous, steamy and totally appealing. Lena Matthews' ability to combine comedy and sinful sexuality in her storylines always leaves me with the satisfaction of reading a terrific story.

~ *Talia Ricci, Joyfully Reviewed*

Joker's Wild: Stripped Bare

Lena Matthews

A Samhain Publishing, Ltd. publication.

Samhain Publishing, Ltd.
512 Forest Lake Drive
Warner Robins, GA 31093
www.samhainpublishing.com

Joker's Wild: Stripped Bare
Copyright © 2007 by Lena Matthews
Print ISBN: 1-59998-627-2
Digital ISBN: 1-59998-187-4

Editing by Jessica Bimberg
Cover by Scott Carpenter

First Samhain Publishing, Ltd. electronic publication: February 2007
First Samhain Publishing, Ltd. print publication: January 2008

Dedication

To Janette—for all of your inspiration, encouragement, and friendship. Thank you for sharing your dream man with me. I hope I made him everything you wished for.

Prologue

"Pencils up, everyone, time's up." A loud, collective groan filled the classroom as students quickly filled in the last few remaining circles on the test sheets. "When I said pencils up, I meant the lead-pointing ends as well," Professor Brody Kincaid said dryly from the front of the room.

This was his last class for the semester, so he was just as anxious to get out of there as the students were to get a few extra minutes to write. Looking across the room at the clock, Brody estimated the time it would take to wrap this up, get home and relax with some soft rock and a nice stiff scotch. Teaching adults was supposed to be easier than teaching kids, but most of the students in his classroom were little more than children themselves.

There were a few sprinkles of gray on several heads, which was a refreshing change, because it made him feel like people were taking his class not just for credit, but to learn. Teaching the willing was a lot more rewarding than teaching the sheep, who were only there because they thought it was an easy A. Renaissance Literature wasn't a hard subject if you liked to read, but finding a person who liked to read in this instant-gratification world was like trying to find a virgin in high school. They were out there but you had to look hard.

Sitting on the edge of his desk, he peered out over the room, looking for anyone still trying to write. As usual, his gaze fell on the slightly bent head of Melissa Haddan, who was putting her closed book into her book bag. Her chestnut-brown hair was pulled up and out of the way, clearing her face of unnecessary debris. Her cool, polished demeanor only made him want to see her ruffled and disheveled. Brody wanted to see her above him, sweaty and free. The thought made him lower the papers he held to cover his stirring erection.

"Could everyone pass their test up to the front of the row and down to the left?" he instructed the waiting faces. Standing up, he walked to the podium and began regurgitating his end-of-the-semester speech. "I hope this class challenged you, and that you got as much out of it as I got from teaching it to you. Your test grade will be posted on the door on Friday, along with your grade for the class. Remember your numbers, because it won't be under your last name. Any questions, I'll be in my office on Tuesday from eleven to three, and if you want to make an appointment for another time, call my office."

Brody raised his eyebrow expectantly. "That's it, people, get out."

Laughing, everyone stood up and rushed to the head of the class. Several female students clamored for his attention, but he only had eyes for one. The one who was standing on the edge of the group, looking around at his fan club.

Not wanting to call attention to herself, she always played down her looks. In her normal late-night school attire, she hid her voluptuous figure behind baggy shirts and jeans. Brody wanted nothing more than to pull her top off and lavish her body with kisses. She reminded him of pin-up girls of the fifties, those full-figured, beautiful women who dominated the screen with their presence and aura.

Brody wanted her to stay, and he discreetly tried to catch her eye. Melissa wasn't one of the academic groupies who got their kicks from fucking professors. In fact, she was the complete opposite. Quiet and reserved, never raising her hand or staying after to ask him questions, she was almost a mirage floating in the distance. If she hadn't turned in her work, he would have doubted she was even there.

Melissa seemed shy and, despite her lush figure, delicate. From the first moment he noticed her, he'd felt an urge to protect. Something about the way she carried herself, and the wary look in her eyes, called out to the soldier still in him. It was one of the things that appealed to him about her, that and her full, large breasts.

He had always been a breast man, even as a teenager he had gone for full-figured women, because he loved to bury his face in their mounds. Once, when he was passing out papers, he had managed to catch a glimpse down her blouse as she was bending forward, and that hint of pale white cleavage had frozen him in his tracks.

Brody liked substance more than sex appeal, and that was what put Melissa on his radar. The few times he'd had a moment with her they had never been alone, which was probably a good thing for his career, because the fact that he was her instructor wouldn't have deterred him at all.

He knew if he had ever been given a chance to be alone with the lush beauty, he would have been hard-pressed not to let her hair down and dive between her thighs. He was really looking forward to this semester ending so he could get to know her a little better.

"Professor Kincaid, I wanted to see about setting up an appointment." Carol Palmer, a leggy redhead who had done everything but drop down on her knees and suck his cock, was fingering a gold necklace and smiling up at him as if he were the sun god Ra.

"Just call my office and I'll see what we can do." Brody made a mental note to avoid her call at all costs. There was no way he wanted to be alone with her. He could already see his tenure being tossed out the window.

"Are you going to be teaching next session?" asked the blonde on his left. Brody didn't know her. He wasn't even sure if she was in the class, but he nodded anyway, hoping to avoid being put in a position where he would have to stutter and try to come up with her name.

Sometimes he felt like a piece of meat on display. His buddies would laugh their asses off if they knew how much he hated being at the receiving end of all those lustful glances. At first it was cool, it was even interesting when he was approached by a student for some after-school tutoring that had absolutely nothing to do with his curriculum. He had eaten it up like candy, but then it just got old.

Brody thought he had heard every silly come-on line ever invented, and some not-so-silly ones, but his sexual urges no longer ran his life. Unless he counted the urge he felt for Melissa. But he was going to be smart about this. He had kept his distance all semester long, even when everything inside him cried out for him to take her, he resisted. He wanted their time together to be special, not rushed or hidden from view. He wanted to be able to have her on his arm and proudly say, "This is my woman".

The women in his class seemed to get younger every semester. Their skirts got shorter and the tops tighter, but he knew if he asked any of them to name a great work of fiction, one of them would say *Harry Potter*. Looking over to where Melissa had been standing, he groaned as he saw her ease through the crowd.

"Mel..." He tried calling to her, but he was too late. She was already out the door before he got her name out. "Fuck," he muttered to himself as she slipped away. *Next time*, he thought sourly, *I won't let you get away so easily.*

Chapter One

Three months later

Missy glanced up from her textbook and peeked over the counter, looking for signs of intelligent life forms in need of her help. Intelligent life forms in an adult bookstore, she thought with a giggle, like that was really going to happen. Not that she had anything against the late-night visitors who gifted her with their presence. If it weren't for people shopping for porn and vibrators at ten o'clock at night, she wouldn't have a job. A job she needed and really liked, despite the location and the merchandise.

Glancing at her wristwatch, she mentally gave herself another ten minutes before she would go bang on the doors of the movie booths to rouse the late-night whackers, so they could hurry up and she could close up. Not wanting to interrupt their jerks, she always coughed loudly before hitting the doors. No need to scare someone into spraying accidentally on the screen. Not that she was going to clean it up if they did. She didn't make that much money.

The bell above the door dinged, alerting Missy of customers entering the store. Setting down her book, she pushed her wire-frame glasses up on her small pug nose, turned and smiled as she saw her friend Kayla and another woman entering the store. Walking from behind the counter, she embraced the multicolor-dressed Kayla, who was beaming as usual. Kayla was one of the few people she knew who constantly had a smile on her face.

"Hi, what are you doing here so late?" Missy asked, pulling back.

"We're here to buy an engagement present for Eliza," Kayla said, pulling the other woman forward.

"You're buying her an engagement present here?"

"Hey, it's the gift that keeps on giving."

Laughing, Missy followed them to the vibrator aisle, still keeping a lookout at the counter. She wasn't worried someone might want to make off with a vibrator, because her policy was, if anyone needed a vibrator so badly they had to steal it, then they were welcome to it.

Holding up a large green vibrator, Eliza asked jokingly, "Hmm, when you see this, what comes to mind?"

"Ointment." Laughing, they put it back and picked up something equally graphic and equally amusing.

"Okay, what about this?" Kayla held up a large lava-lamp-shaped butt plug.

"That you have to tweak your nipples to turn it on."

"My theory," Missy said, very dignified-like, "is if you can take something that large in your ass, do you really need it?"

The women burst out laughing at the assortment of gadgets surrounding them. Missy often thought the devices were silly, but it wasn't like she could ask a customer who was buying one what the hell they were thinking.

The bell rang again and she stepped out of the aisle and watched as several well-dressed, tuxedo-clad men entered the building.

"Hubba hubba, ding ding, baby, you got everything," Kayla said, stepping into the aisle, eyeing the gorgeous men.

Elbowing her, Missy muttered, drooling herself, "You're engaged, back off."

"Engaged, honey, not blind."

Smiling, Missy walked behind the counter. Sitting on her stool, she shuffled her feet back and forth, eyeing the men as they strolled down the aisles. There was absolutely nothing sexier in the world than hot men dressed in tuxedos. Nothing.

"Missy," Kayla called from the toy section. "Eliza needs to know which anal plug you would recommend."

Red heat flushed her cheeks as several of the tuxedo-clad men turned in her direction. Ducking her head, she hid her scarlet face behind her hair and hopped off the stool. She was going to kill Kayla, she fumed silently as she hurried from behind the counter. One of the reasons she liked being back there was because it hid her plump figure, which was exactly what she wanted to do when she was in the presence of mouth-watering men. Hide.

"Did you have to yell that?" she muttered to a laughing Kayla.

"Oops, my bad," Kayla teased. Picking up a plug, she said, "Eliza here is working up the nerve to have anal sex—much to the delight of Chris, I might add—and she's looking for a starter kit."

"A starter kit, huh?" Missy's whiskey-brown eyes crinkled in delight. She could see why Kayla liked to tease so much.

"Chris is trying to weasel his way out of my third fantasy, by insisting on this as his reward for fulfilling his end of the bet."

"What bet?" asked Missy.

"Better yet, what was the third fantasy?" Kayla asked.

"Forget I said anything," Eliza remarked, blushing.

"I don't think so," Kayla said, leaning against the dildo display. "Inquiring minds want to know."

"Okay, I'll tell, if you tell about a certain phone call you made a while back."

"Never mind," Kayla muttered, looking down. Her cheeks began to show a hint of pink, which only spurred Missy's curiosity further.

"Why do I feel left out?" she asked, looking at the two women.

"Hey, do you play poker?" quipped Kayla. "Maybe you can come to one of our games."

"No I don't..."

"Excuse me," said a deep masculine voice from behind Missy. Turning around, she looked into the eyes of her former college Renaissance Literature professor, Brody Kincaid. "I would like to be rung up."

"Sure, no problem," Missy said, scampering around him. Walking quickly to the front of the store, she reminded herself it was highly unlikely he would even recognize her. Out of a sea of students, she doubted she stood out. Not one to call attention to herself, she never raised her hand to answer questions and never showed up too early or too late for class. Missy had crafted the art of blending in to a science.

Standing behind the counter, she studied him while he put his items down. Dressed like the other men who had walked in, he was wearing a tuxedo without the tie, with the first few buttons undone. His black hair was full and thick and lightly touched the collar of his shirt. In a word, he was delicious.

Ringing up his purchases, she tried hard not to notice what he bought, but that was like trying not to stare at an accident. Missy really wanted to know, though, why a man that attractive needed a blow-up doll and handcuffs. It wasn't like the doll was going to go anywhere, but working here she had seen stranger things.

"So, Melissa Haddan, should I worry you're going to try to use this to change your grade on your transcripts?" he teased as she picked up the pussy lollipops.

Looking up quickly, she gazed, startled, into his large gray eyes. She was surprised he had even noticed her, let alone knew who she was. "Umm, of course not, sir," she stuttered as she shoved the pussies into the bag.

"I was joking," he assured her, making her blush brighter. "I'm just surprised to see you here."

"I guess I could say the same."

Chuckling, he nodded his head in agreement. "Touché, Ms. Haddan. But see, I could always use the bachelor party as my excuse."

"Well, then, I guess I'll just use the need to pay my bills as mine." Missy wasn't used to men paying her this much attention. The way he was looking at her made her feel warm and itchy. Like her skin didn't fit. It was very unsettling, but felt oddly good at the same time.

Stepping back from the counter, he looked down the row of impulse items, and selected a pair of racy playing cards. Tossing them on the counter, he reached in his jacket pocket and pulled out his wallet.

"Did I hear correctly, you don't know how to play poker?"

"Yes."

"That's a shame. I happen to be a poker aficionado."

"Really?"

"Yes."

"I know. It's sad, isn't it? I've always wanted to play, but never had the time to learn."

"There's always time," he said, handing her the money.

"Why do you say that?"

"I'd be more than willing to teach you."

"Oh, I don't know." Missy hesitated. "That's probably not a good idea."

"Anthony Holden said, 'Whether he likes it or not, a man's character is stripped bare at the poker table; if the other players read him better than he does, he has only himself to blame. Unless he is both able and prepared to see himself as others do, flaws and all, he will be a loser in cards, as in life.' And I would have to say I wholeheartedly agree. There's a science to it, an art if you dare, but truly, when it comes down to it, it's all about how well you know yourself and how far you're willing to go."

Missy felt the urge to look behind her, to make sure the looks of interest she thought he was sending were really for her. Reaching into the register, Missy took out his change, praying it was the right amount. Feeling flustered, she thrust the money at him. Brody lightly brushed his fingers against hers as he took the money. Her pulse tattooed beneath her skin, joining the erratic beat of her heart.

Brody's gaze flickered to her mouth as she licked her lips nervously, before swinging back to her eyes. He reached into his wallet and pulled out a business card and slid it across the counter towards her. Picking up his bag, he asked her. "How far are you willing to go, Melissa?"

Blushing, Missy looked down at the card on the counter and watched from her peripheral vision as he joined the rest of his party and walked out of the store. Missy stared down at the card as if she was afraid that it was going to jump up and bite her. Reaching slowly for it, she grazed the corner just as Kayla swiped it from under her fingertips.

"What's this?" Kayla demanded eagerly.

"Nothing," Missy said, snatching the card out of her hand. Sliding it in her pocket, she eyed them over the counter warily and asked, "Are you ready to check out?"

"Not until I hear what that hottie..."

"Kayla, you're embarrassing her. Not everyone is as enthusiastic about sharing their love life as you are." Eliza smiled sympathetically at Missy.

"Ahhh, come on, just a little dirt," begged Kayla.

"He's my old professor," Missy admitted, giving in to her. She adored Kayla, but she wasn't quite comfortable sharing personal information with her. Especially when she wasn't sure what she thought of the brief encounter. Men like Professor Kincaid didn't look twice at big girls like her.

"What, did you forget to turn in an assignment? Is he going to make you stay after?" Kayla teased.

Ringing up the anal kit, she tried to block out Kayla's harmless comment. She knew Kayla didn't mean anything by it, but it still made her uncomfortable.

"How about we wait until you're done and we can go to Denny's and grab a milkshake?" Kayla offered.

The idea of downing a shake with these two beautiful women made her stomach turn. There was no way she was eating, let alone eating ice cream with these two. Her fragile ego couldn't handle it and neither could her diet.

"I'd love to," she lied. "But I have a mound of homework waiting for me at home."

"Can't it wait?" pouted Kayla.

"Yes, please," Eliza asked.

"No, but I would love a rain check."

"Sure." Looking downhearted, Kayla picked up the discreet black bag and handed it to Eliza. "But I will keep you to that."

"I hope so." Missy smiled. Looking at Eliza, she said, "It was nice to meet you."

"You too," Eliza replied.

Looking down at her watch, Missy groaned as she noticed the time. Walking through the aisle, she turned the corner and headed down the hallway, coughing loudly before saying, "We'll be closing in five minutes."

Heading back to the counter, she straightened up while waiting for the store to empty. Missy made a final closing call over the loudspeaker and watched as the last Looky Lous left the store before doing her final walk down the aisle. After locking the doors, she tallied the register and placed the money in the safe.

Opening the hall closet, she took out the vacuum and ran it quickly over the carpet. She wanted to hurry up and get home so she could work on her paper. After finishing all of her closing chores, Missy reached in her pocket for the keys and halted when she felt her hand close around the card Professor Kincaid had given her.

Pulling it out of her pocket, she looked at the card that gave his name, his office hours and phone number. Missy wondered what the hell he could have been thinking to give her this. He was a good-looking man, she thought as she shoved the card back in her pocket. What would he want with her? She normally wasn't this negative, but she was always realistic.

Brody could have anyone he wanted, including her, but that didn't explain why he would be interested. Pulling the door closed behind her, Missy locked it and walked to her car. Getting in, she sat for a moment staring at the neon "closed" sign in the window of Harris's. Missy took his card out again, balled it up and threw it on the floor of her car. She had a lot going for herself these days, too much to be getting caught up in his game.

Brody watched the stripper with blank eyes. All he could do was think back to earlier that night when he ran into Melissa at Harris's. You could have knocked him over with a feather when he realized who she was. She was the last person he would have ever expected to find in an adult bookstore.

Candy, or whatever her real name was, dropped into his lap and gyrated her bony ass against his lap, hoping for a reaction. Ignoring the catcalls of his friends, he pushed her up and stood. Leaving the party, he walked onto the balcony of the hotel and pulled a cigarette out of his jacket pocket. Lighting it, he inhaled the nicotine deep and held it there. Slowly releasing it, he blew the smoke, along with his frustration, into the chilly night air.

The sliding door opened behind him, blasting the silence with loud music and bawdy language. Looking over his shoulder, Brody smiled at a fellow groomsman, his brother Bryce.

"The party too much for you?" asked Bryce, taking the cigarette out of his hand and tossing it over the balcony.

"No, but who hired the stripper? I'm fighting the need to feed and clothe her with everything inside of me," Brody replied dryly.

Laughing, Bryce smiled up at him. He and his brother shared the same preferences when it came to women, full and feminine. "Well, you know I didn't," he teased.

Grinning, Brody stared back into the star-filled night. He knew, as best man, he should be in there ensuring their cousin Jake had the time of his life, but he just couldn't get the image of Melissa surrounded by toys out of his head.

"So what's the story with you and the clerk?" Bryce asked, leaning on the railing beside him.

"There isn't one. She's a former student of mine."

"Is that all?"

"For now."

"I know that tone." Bryce tipped his beer bottle up, saluting his brother. "Keep in mind, brother, anything worth doing is worth doing slowly."

Snorting, Brody looked over at him and laughed. "You can't possibly be related to me."

"That's what I kept telling Mom, but she denies it."

"I have a feeling if I go too slowly with her she'll end up running." Looking over the balcony, Brody stared down into the crowded parking lot. "And I'm not going to let her get away."

"This time or ever?"

Brody turned and looked his brother in his eyes, all trace of kidding gone. "What do you think?"

"I think if she's going to run, she better start now."

Chapter Two

Closing the car door behind him, Brody slid on his sunglasses and strolled through the parking lot of the campus, dodging students and fellow faculty alike. Tightening his hold on his leather satchel, he weaved through the crowded sidewalk, eyes darting back and forth in search for a particular familiar face.

Ever since Saturday night, he had been waiting very impatiently for a phone call from Melissa. He hoped he might have piqued her interest, because Lord knows that after first seeing her last semester she had piqued his. He was more than a little irked she hadn't gotten in contact with him, but he wasn't going to let it dissuade him.

Nodding his head to a smiling student, Brody strolled through the campus, destination unknown. Lost in his thoughts, he was oblivious to the wanton stares aimed in his direction from the majority of the female population. A man confident with his looks, Brody was well aware of his appeal, but it wasn't something he allowed to go to his head. The old adage of "pretty is as pretty does" was as true today as when it was first murmured.

Walking to the center of the campus, where many of the students hung out, he stood at the top of the stairs and peered through the mass of people, searching for a glimpse of Melissa. Narrowing his eyes, he meticulously filtered the different faces from his view until his gaze landed on a bent head under a tree. The brown hair, held up in a ponytail, was similar to the color and style of Melissa's, as was the slope of the shoulders shielding her from prying eyes.

As if feeling his stare, Melissa looked up and scanned her surroundings. Raising her hand, she placed it over her eyes, shielding the glare from the sun as she turned her head, looking around. Brody stood where he was, waiting to see if she would notice him, but her gaze brushed past him as if she didn't see him. It somewhat annoyed him that her eyes weren't drawn to him as his were to her. He wanted to overwhelm her senses as she'd done to him. To be the only person she thought of all day, like he thought of her. Intent on garnering her attention, Brody walked down the stairs, planning to approach her, when a man flopped down next to her and yanked the book from her hands.

Frowning, Brody watched their interplay with annoyance. He didn't like the way she smiled at the other man, and he definitely didn't like the implied familiarity she had with him. The thought that she might be taken had never occurred to him. It wasn't as if he were surprised anyone else might find her attractive, because that certainly wasn't the case, but the idea of someone else having a prior claim to her didn't sit well with him.

As Brody got closer to the tree, Melissa looked up again and saw him. Her surprise at seeing him flashed quickly across her face before she gathered herself together. Her companion looked up as well, and Brody recognized him from one his classes.

"Ms. Haddan," Brody said, nodding at her. Turning, he addressed the man with her. "Scott Nelson, right?"

"Yeah, I'm in your lit class," Scott said, holding out his hand.

Shaking it firmly, Brody resisted the childish urge to squeeze his hand hard. He wasn't going to act like a jealous fool until it was time to.

"I was expecting a call from you," Brody said, turning to look back at Melissa.

Her skin darkened in a slightly red flush. "I misplaced your card."

Brody wasn't sure if she was lying or not, but he was willing to give her the benefit of the doubt.

"I didn't know you were taking his class this semester," Scott stated, looking between the two of them, confused.

"I'm not," she murmured softly, looking down.

"Then why..." He stopped and turned in surprise to look at Brody.

Scott's amazement made Brody want to shove his fist down the young man's throat. Why would Scott be so surprised that Brody was interested in Melissa? Flushing more, Melissa seemed to catch on to his surprise, which angered Brody further.

"If you have time now, Ms. Haddan, I would love to continue our discussion in my office. I'm free until two."

"I have class in half an hour," she stated.

"It shouldn't take that long." He waited, staring down at her. Melissa frowned slightly and nodded her head.

Tossing the books together in her bag, she placed her hand on the ground to push herself up and froze when Brody held out his hand. Ignoring his gesture, she said, "That's okay, I can do it."

Bending forward, he took the hand that was on her backpack and pulled gently until she was standing up.

"You could have hurt yourself."

Throwing back his head, he laughed at her comment. "By you, I seriously doubt it."

Melissa looked at him, confused, before turning to Scott. "I'll talk to you later."

"Call me later."

"'Kay."

Walking away from the tree, they headed down the sidewalk to his office. They walked in silence for several minutes before Brody's curiosity got the better of him. "Is he your boyfriend?"

"Who, Scott?" she asked, bewildered.

"Yes."

A huge grin spread across her pretty face, crinkling her eyes behind her glasses. She looked so damn adorable he wanted to stop right then and there and kiss her.

"No." She laughed, smiling up at him. "I'm not his type."

"Is he gay?"

That caused a bigger laugh to escape from between her full lips. "Not hardly, I'm just not his cup of tea."

"Do you want to be?"

"No." She smiled. "We're just really good friends."

Nodding, he opened the outside door for her and gestured her down the long hall. "So what is his type?"

"He likes the famished look."

Smiling, he stopped at his office and unlocked the door. Slipping his hand in, Brody turned on the light and held the door open. Shutting the door behind them, he gestured for her to take a seat in the cushioned swivel chair in front of his desk. Brody took off his jacket and hung it, along with his satchel, on the coat rack before he turned and faced her.

"So what's the real reason you didn't call me?" he asked, walking around the desk to sit on the corner facing her.

"I misplaced your card."

"It wouldn't have been hard to find me," he stated, looking down at her. "I was able to find out you were at school today."

"How did you?"

"I called Harris's and asked to speak to you. They said you had class today, so I came in early."

"Why?"

"Because I wanted to see you."

"All of this because you wanted to teach me poker?"

"Among other things, yes."

Squinting her eyes, she asked suspiciously, "What things?"

"Whatever you want to learn."

Crossing her arms over her chest, she sat back in her chair and stared at him. "Why do I feel we're not talking cards here?"

"Well, I'm not."

"Then what are you talking about?" she asked.

"What do you think?"

Standing, Melissa pushed back her chair. "Look, Professor Kincaid..."

"Brody."

"Fine, is this some kind of game?"

"Of course not, Melissa."

"It's Missy, all right?"

"Missy." He nodded, testing the name on his lips. He liked it. It suited her, he thought with a smile. She was being so fierce, but he could tell by the way her nipples were protruding against her pink shirt that she wasn't as oblivious as she was pretending to be. "I'm not playing a game with you. I want to get to know you. Is that so hard to believe?"

"Yes, as a matter of fact it is."

"Why?"

"Oh come on. You have to own a mirror," she replied sarcastically.

"So what, you don't go out with guys with dark hair?"

"I don't go out with guys, period."

"If you tell me you're a lesbian, I might just drop dead," he joked, reaching out to push a stray hair off her face.

"I'm not a lesbian." She frowned. "I'm fat. And you're beautiful."

Brody stood, frowning down at her. "You're not fat, and I don't like you saying that."

"Tough," she said, stepping back from him. "It's true, and if you can't deal with it, that's your problem."

"No, my dear, it's yours." Stepping closer to her, Brody pushed the chair away from her and grabbed her hand. Pulling her closer to him, he looked down into her upturned face and said, "If you ever say that again, I'm going to show you how much of a problem it will be for you. You're not fat, you're beautiful."

Rolling her eyes, she tried to snatch back her hand but couldn't. "Look, Brody, you don't have to take me on as a project. I'm not some low-self-esteem girl that needs rescuing by a handsome man. I don't need a pity fuck. I'm a big girl, I can handle the truth."

"How's this for some truth?" he growled, pulling her hand down to his hardening crotch. Pushing it against his erection, he bent forward and kissed her hard. His mouth captured hers and forced her lips apart with his thrusting tongue. Moaning, Missy kissed him back, slipping her tongue around his.

Brody pulled back, "I know you're a big girl." Running his hand up to her breast, he squeezed her full mound, pinching her erect nipple in the process. "That's one of the things I like about you."

He spun her around and pushed her against the wall, pressing his hard cock into her backside. Brody leaned forward and began to nibble on the side of her neck. He worked his way up to her cheek, ending with a light but firm bite on her earlobe. "If you ever call yourself fat again in my presence, I'm going to tan this delectable backside of yours."

"You and what army?" she asked heatedly.

Pushing his hand around the front of her, Brody kneaded her breasts as he pressed into her from behind. Rubbing his hard cock around her ass must have been having the same effect on her as it was on him, because her nipples were erect and her breathing erratic.

"Baby, I'm a one-man army." He bit down on her shoulder blade. She cried out in pleasure as he slipped his other hand down her stomach and palmed her pussy. Squeezing it, he gripped her and pulled her back harder onto him. Moving his fingers up the seam, he unbuckled and unzipped her pants, working quickly to prevent any arguments.

Slipping his hand inside her cotton panties, Brody fingered her wet clit. Missy pushed back against him, arching her breasts as he worked a finger up her wet hole.

"Look how wet for me you are," he murmured into her ear. "You're eating my hand up with this wet pussy. I can't wait to bury my cock in you."

Groaning, Missy rocked against him and Brody felt her body begin to tremble. He wondered if she was going to get off from this simple contact, and pressed his palm against her swollen clit, pushing against it as he added another finger inside her.

"Are you going to come, baby?"

"Ye...yes," she gushed, riding his hand.

"Good, I want you to." Pushing into her harder, he rubbed against her ass and sped up the rhythm of his hand. "Fuck my hand, baby. Ride it until you come against me."

"Brody... I..." A knock interrupted her response, and her body tightened up around him. Uncaring, Brody squeezed her nipple harder and rubbed his palm against her clit.

"No," he whispered in her ear. "You come for me."

Missy raised her hand up to push him away, but Brody shoved another finger into her at the same time. "Come for me now," he demanded as her body rocked and flooded his hand with juices. Throwing her head back, Missy bit down on her bottom lip to stifle her groan. She shook from the force of her climax, and he held her tightly to him as the person knocked against the door again.

"Professor Kincaid, are you there?" inquired a female voice from outside the door.

Stiffening against him, Missy looked over her shoulder at him and waited for his reply. "I'll be right there," he said through clenched teeth.

Pushing away, Missy righted her clothes and turned angrily to him. "Is she getting a card lesson also?"

"Still tense, I see." He brought his wet fingers to his mouth. "Do you want to go again? I'll get rid of her."

"Don't do me any favors."

Frowning, Brody stared at her. "Do you any favors? I'm the one still hard here!"

"Maybe she can help you out."

"I don't want her, I want you. Or do I need to prove it to you again?"

Flushing, she gathered her books and headed to the door.

"Missy," he called out softly behind her.

"What?" she said, her hand on the doorknob.

"This isn't over."

Looking over her shoulder at him, she replied, "I didn't think it was," before opening the door and walking out.

Chapter Three

The dinging of the bell brought Missy out of her self-imposed stupor. She was still reeling from the hand-to-hand combat with Brody this afternoon, so much so that she wasn't even sure how she managed to get to work. Not that she had to be all there to ring up dildos, but it would help if she could at least focus on her medical terms. No one was going to hire anyone who didn't know the difference between URI and UTI.

Sighing, she closed the book and set it down on the bottom counter. The rest of her day was completely shot because of him. If she didn't get her shit together and soon, she was never going to get into medical school. It was a lifetime goal that had taken many months of skimping on everything from food to new clothes, just so she could save up for school. If it weren't for this job, she would still be bussing tables and taking a class once a week at the local community college.

It might not be the most conventional place to work but it suited her just fine. Dean Harris, the owner, allowed her to work around her school schedule and didn't complain when she asked for days off. Despite its products and sometimes strange customers, Harris's was an ideal place to work.

Climbing down from the stool, she picked up the duster and walked around the counter. Barely touching the shelf, she grazed the surface of the table, the feathers teasing the dust as she drifted down the row. Visions of this afternoon ran in her head, leaving her to ponder what the hell she had been thinking.

It wasn't like her to be so free with her body, not that Brody had given her much say in the matter. He came, he saw, he conquered. Okay, so she came, but he had definitely conquered. She had been such an easy target. He had just swooped down and pounced, and all of her free will had vanished. Not that he'd done anything she hadn't wanted, it was just that he was so overpowering.

Brody's sexual prowess far outweighed the meager bump and grind she had experienced in her past. And after Tony, her ex, she was a little gun-shy. Which, mingled with her regular shy personality, left her feeling like an invisible mound of mush. There was no way Brody could ever be interested in her. The cute, great guy only fell for the homely, fat chicks in bad TV movies.

The door swinging open wildly sent the bell into an epileptic seizure. Glancing up, she watched in surprise as Brody strolled into the store. In form-fitting blue jeans and a gray short-sleeved shirt, he appeared as if she conjured him out of her fantasy. Every time she watched him move, she heard hot jazz music playing in the back of her head. As if she was mentally playing a song for him to strip to. The thought of him naked and shaking his moneymaker made her blush from the sheer vision of him.

"I would say a penny for your thoughts, but the way you're blushing, I'd be willing to pay a hell of a lot more," he teased, strolling up to her. His stormy gray eyes twinkled in merriment.

Blushing brighter, Missy cringed at his knowing laugh and wished the ground would just open up and swallow her whole. The scent of his cologne drifted up to her and doused her senses with a direct hit of pheromones. The aroma, rich and spicy and with a hint of his own unique scent, soared around her, forcing Missy to grip the feather duster to prevent herself from attacking him and dragging him to the floor.

"You know stalking is illegal in the state of California," she quipped, once she was able to gather her ability to think.

Grinning, Brody replied, "Well, if the mountain won't come to Muhammad..."

"Comparing me to a mountain won't get you far, Muhammad."

"Sounds to me like someone is trying to call herself fat in a roundabout way."

"No, I wasn't," she denied. "But if I wanted to, I would."

"I wouldn't advise it if I were you," Brody threatened softly. His commanding tone caught her off guard, as did her urge to obey him. Something about his presence stilled her automatic response sensors.

Joker's Wild: Stripped Bare

"What are you doing here?" she asked, walking around the counter. Missy wanted to put as much distance between them as she could.

"I came to see you," he answered, leaning against the counter. "We have some unfinished business, you and I."

"Look, this afternoon I wasn't myself."

"So who was it that squeezed my fingers like a vise-grip in my office this afternoon?"

Missy's eyes widened. She flushed, feeling the heat spread up from her breasts to her cheeks. Looking over his shoulder, Missy glanced around to see if any of the few customers who were nearby heard him.

Leaning forward, she whispered hotly, "Don't talk about that here."

"I can't talk about sex in a sex shop?"

"We didn't have sex and no, you can't. This is my place of employment."

"My purpose isn't to embarrass you, Missy," he chided softly, "but to try to get to know you better."

"Know me better?" she questioned in shock. "You don't know me at all."

"Oh, I beg to differ, little one. I know enough."

"Because I took your class?"

"No, because I tasted you." Running his hands over the counter, he brushed the tips of his fingers against the soft flesh of her arm. "I want more than a taste now; I want the whole damn meal."

Pulling back her arm, she looked at Brody, not quite sure what to say. There was no use trying to act blasé with him. She could no more pull off the seductress act than he could act like a choirboy. Missy was way out of her element, and she knew it.

"Stop looking at me like that," he said, reaching over the counter for her hand. Pulling it forward, he caressed her palm as if he was trying to calm a skittish mare. "What are you afraid of?"

"You," she said stiffly. "You're going to run all over me."

"That's not my intention."

"But you'll do it anyway. I'm not equipped to handle you."

"What do you mean?" Brody tilted his head and smiled gently at her.

"You're going to try to turn this into a sex thing."

"And that would be bad, why?"

"Because look at you and look at me."

"I am looking, Missy."

Frustrated, she yanked her hand away and stepped back from the counter. "No, look at me, Brody."

"I am looking," he said firmly. "And I like what I see."

"You're confusing me."

"What's confusing about me wanting to get to know you better?" Brody asked, shaking his head in bewilderment.

"You're going too fast."

"I'll slow down."

Missy tried to read his intent with a slight frown on her face. He appeared to be sincere, but she couldn't be sure. She was still waiting for her bullshit meter to start going off. When something appeared to be too good to be true, it was normally because it was.

"Really." He laughed at her disbelieving stare. "We can start off as friends."

"Well, I normally don't let my friends finger me in their offices."

"Where do you let them finger you?"

"I didn't mean..." She flushed, feeling foolish and embarrassed. "I don't let them finger me at all."

"Damn," Brody teased. "And here I was looking forward to the benefits of being your friend."

"You're going to make me have an aneurysm from all this blood rushing to my head."

"Stop blushing, then. You don't have to be embarrassed with me."

"I do if you want me to be myself."

A customer walked up to the counter, shooting Brody a strange look. Stepping back, Brody waved the man forward and browsed the novelty aisle as she waited on the customer.

Missy rang him up, keeping an eye on Brody. Many of her friends visited her at work, mainly for sport, but no one had come just to hang out with her. It was disconcerting, the attention he was paying her, but nice at the same time.

When her customer left, Brody came back to the counter with two jars in his hands. Placing them on the counter in front of her, he asked, "So, miss, which anal lube do you recommend?"

Missy looked from him to the jars, trying to gauge if he was serious or not. "I think lube is a personal decision."

"But you work here; you must have a personal favorite." If it weren't for the twinkle in his eyes, she would have thought by his tone that he was serious.

"Well sure, I guess it depends on if it's *your* anus that we're talking about."

"No, it's for a friend."

"That's some kind of friend."

"That's what I keep saying." A huge grin split Brody's face, and Missy had to chuckle despite herself.

"The KY is the best-selling one."

"Okay, then I'll take it."

"Big date planned?"

"No, but you can never have too much lube." He winked as he took the other jar off the counter. Walking back down the aisle, he picked up a deck of cards, featuring nude people, and tossed them to her. "I'll take these too."

"I'm not learning poker on these cards." Missy wrinkled her nose in distaste, looking down at the graphic deck. "I think the queen in here might actually *be* a queen, and I'm not talking the Elizabeth variety."

Grinning, Brody caught the cards in mid-air as she tossed them back at him. "You have to be open-minded."

"I'm very open-minded, but this deck brings a whole other image to mind when you say one-eyed jacks."

Brody threw back his head and roared with laughter. Smiling with mirth, Missy watched him, pleased. Once she got over his devastating good looks, and the fact that he'd brought her to orgasm against a wall, she would be able to treat him like she did her other male friends. Maybe if she just put him in the friend box, she could get a grip on her hormones and go back to being herself.

"So are you really interested in teaching me poker?" she asked, coming from behind the counter.

"Of course. Do you want to learn?"

"Very much so." Walking around to the opposite aisle, she stood with the shelves between them.

"What about tonight, you want to go back to my house?" Raising his hands in mock surrender, he added, "Or yours, wherever you feel most comfortable."

"We don't close until eleven," Missy stated. Biting down on her bottom lip, she waited for his response. Reaching over the shelves, he ran his thumb over her lip, gently moving it from between her teeth. The feel of his thick finger against her mouth had her nipples tightening under her loose-fitting shirt.

"I'm free tonight," he said softly, taking his thumb away from her slightly opened lips.

Licking them, Missy felt a tingle run through her body. "I have class tomorrow at three."

"I won't stay too late."

"Are you sure?"

"Definitely."

"Okay, do you want to meet me back here at closing time?"

"It's only an hour away. I'll wait."

Wrinkling her brow, she asked, "You're just going to hang out here for an hour?"

"Missy," he said teasingly. "I'm surrounded by lube, toys and porn. Why would I wait anywhere else?"

"If you open it, you buy it." Missy smiled, teasing back. This was so out of character for her. She hadn't blushed in five minutes. It had to be a new record, she thought sarcastically. She could do this; she could be friends with him, if he stopped touching her that is. Because when he did, she lost the last of the common sense God gave her, and wanted to body-check him and put the lube to good use.

"I'll keep that in mind." Looking around the store, he asked, "Is it always this quiet here?"

"You've probably scared some people away."

Turning back to her, he asked, "Why would you say that?"

"No one wants other people to see them buying this stuff."

"But you're here."

"Who cares what I think? I work here, but you, well, you're another matter all together."

"Because..."

"Because some people find it embarrassing to buy porn or lube in front of other people," she explained mockingly. "Not everyone is as comfortable with themselves as you appear to be."

"What about you?"

"What about me, what?"

"Could you buy something in front of me?"

"I don't know," Missy tilted her head as she thought. "Normally I would say no, but I did ring you up for a blow-up doll and handcuffs. Not to mention the lube you're buying tonight, so maybe."

"What would you buy?" he inquired curiously.

"I said maybe, it was a hypothetical question."

"Well, hypothetically, what toy here has your interest?"

Rolling her eyes, she said, "That's like asking someone who works in fast food what you should order. They don't eat the stuff there anymore, it's old news. Same thing here. I've had to log, order and stock all these things. The novelty of it all is lost on me."

"Well, if not a toy, what?"

"I don't know," she hedged.

"Just pick one thing. What would it be?"

"Well, it wouldn't be a toy."

"Okay, what would it be?"

"I don't know, maybe a movie."

"What kind?"

"The dirty kind." He was enjoying this conversation way too much for her peace of mind.

"Any particular kind of dirty movie?" he inquired dryly.

"Are you trying to make me blush again?"

"Are you trying to avoid the question?"

"No."

"Then answer it." Crossing his arms across his chest, he raised an eyebrow as if daring her.

"I don't know, maybe something with…" Reaching up, Missy tugged on her ponytail. This was definitely not the kind of conversation she had with Scott. "A threesome maybe." Missy mumbled the last part, hoping like hell that her face wasn't as red as it felt.

"Ahh," he said, nodding his head slowly. "Interested in that, are you?"

"No," Missy denied, resisting the urge to touch the tip of her nose, to check to see if it was growing. "I've just never seen one, and I'm curious about it merely from the 'how does it work' factor."

"Really?" It looked as if Brody was holding back laughing at her. "From an instructor viewpoint, I would have to say that knowledge is power."

"Ha, ha, ha," she remarked snidely, stepping back behind the counter when another customer came up from the back of the store.

Brody disappeared around the corner as she waited on the customer. Ringing him up, she wondered what Brody was up to, but she had several customers come up and was unable to go investigate. As the last customer left, Brody appeared with a box in his hand.

Coming up to the counter he smiled and handed it to her. "I would like to purchase this along with the lube."

Looking down, Missy did a double take when she saw the cover of the box. It was a movie cover with a picture of a nude woman on it, giving head to one well-endowed man while getting fucked from behind by another. "What's this for?"

"I believe in being prepared."

"For what?"

"For whatever," he said, pulling out his wallet.

"I thought tonight was about poker."

"It is. Tonight is about poker." Brody handed her his credit card and she just gripped it, still in shock. "Tomorrow, though, is another story."

Chapter Four

Brody followed Missy's red Honda Civic closely, making sure he didn't get lost. Teaching her poker wasn't the way he wanted to necessarily spend the night, but anything that got him alone with her was okay with him. They had spent the last hour at the store, laughing and joking around. Missy had begun to loosen up and feel more comfortable with him the more he backed off and gave her some space. She was like a skittish colt, nervous and untrusting, but Brody was willing to take things as slow as she wanted, as long as she agreed to see him.

He'd never had to pursue a woman in his life. It was a very humbling and irritating feeling. Missy was definitely worth the wait, even if she didn't think she was. He'd just have to take matters into his own hands until she was ready to go further. He would give her time, but not too much. Brody didn't want her to get so comfortable that he fell off her sensual radar and straight into her friend one. He was okay with being friends, as long as it was friends with benefits—the horizontal kind.

Pulling up next to the curb behind her car, he turned off the engine and looked around. The dark night sky seemed like an eerie backdrop to the destitute street leading to the perilous-looking apartment building Missy obviously lived in. There were a few streetlights on, casting an even gloomier glow on her home.

Getting out of the car, he locked his door and set his alarm, something he hardly ever did. Walking behind Missy, who waited for him at the curb, he wondered how she managed to make it home safely every night. There were no security guards to patrol the grounds. No one to make sure she made it into her home unharmed. The thought of her vulnerable to anyone and everyone made his stomach clench. His protective instinct kicked into overdrive as he walked up the stairs behind her.

Brody was so distracted by listening to sounds and peering into the dark that he didn't get to relish the sight of her full ass inches from his face as she trotted up the stairs in front of him. When they reached the second floor apartments, Missy turned down the dim hall and walked up to one of the only apartments with a light working outside the door. Watching behind them as she opened the door, Brody rushed her in as soon as the door was unlocked.

"Be it ever so humble," Missy said, turning on the light by the door. Taking off her jacket, she dropped it on a dowdy plaid loveseat near the door. She turned on more lights the farther into the apartment she went, brightening the dark place up.

Brody looked around the room and was surprised by what he saw. The apartment wasn't very large, but what she lacked in space she made up with in style. It was very simple yet very inviting, much like the owner. The living room opened up into a small kitchen and there was a small hallway off to the side. Her walls were white, but had pictures adorning them. It was neat, warm and a complete contrast to the exterior.

Although the furniture was obviously secondhand, Missy made the dismal apartment as cozy as any home he had ever been in. An oak side table with a black lamp separated the red plaid couches. She had a small coffee table in front, facing an armoire, which housed the entertainment unit.

"Would you like something to drink?" she asked, standing in the kitchen.

"A beer if you have it," Brody said, walking over to her. Sitting at the small round dining table, he watched her bend over and peer in the refrigerator.

Standing up, Missy smiled widely as she held a beer over her head triumphantly. "You're in luck. Scott must have left it here."

Brody accepted the beer grudgingly. He didn't like the idea of Scott being in her apartment, let alone having something of his here, even something as silly as a beer. "Does he come over here often?"

"Fairly often, I guess," she said, riffling through a kitchen drawer. "We study a lot together."

Snorting, Brody opened the bottle and took a long swig. He hoped the bastard died of thirst the next time he was here. "Is he a nursing major as well?"

Turning around, Missy looked at him curiously. "How did you know I was majoring in nursing?"

"I have connections."

"I think that's illegal."

"Legal, illegal, it's all separated by a fine line," Brody said, holding his fingers a mere inch apart.

"What else did you find out about me?" she asked, placing her hands on her hips.

"That you're twenty-six, a straight-A student." Smirking, he added, "And your middle name is Mildred."

"Oh my God." Missy closed her eyes and cringed. Shaking her head, she opened her eyes and said, "You know I have to kill you now, right?"

Laughing, he stood up and crossed his arms. "Do you think you could take me?" he asked cockily.

Tilting her head to the side, Missy studied him. "Maybe. I've been working out."

"Now I'm scared."

"You should be," she teased. Turning her back to him, she opened up another drawer and cheered. "Woo hoo! I found them."

Holding a deck of cards, she turned around and smiled. Her smile lit her entire face. Small laugh lines crinkled next to her eyes, almost hidden behind her wire-framed glasses. Brody had to resist the urge to pull her close to him and kiss her. He wanted to hold her close, to feel the weight of her body against his.

Dropping the cards on the table, Missy walked to the side of the couch and opened her book bag. Pulling out a notebook and a pen, she sat down across from him at the table.

"Okay, let's start with the basics," she said, opening the notebook to a blank page and looking up at him seriously. Picking up her pen, she waited expectedly.

Brody smiled at her and picked up the deck. He should have known Missy would take this as seriously as she did everything. Brody didn't doubt for a minute she would be a quick study, because she seemed to excel at everything she did.

"Let's start with five card stud," he said as he shuffled the cards. He grinned discreetly as Missy quickly jotted down what he said. Brody cleared his throat, trying to erase all elements of amusement from it. "It's probably the easiest to learn. I deal five cards and you try to come up with the best hand possible. Depending on the house rules, you may have to start off with an ante before you even see your hand, or after you see your hand, you have to make the first wager."

"Wait," Missy demanded, hopping up from her seat. She left the room for a moment, only to return seconds later with a small water jug filled with change. Dumping it onto the table, she separated all the change and divided it equally between them. Smiling proudly, she said, "Okay, now we can start."

Shaking his head amusedly, he dealt out five cards, face down. "Write this down, this is the order of highest rank. Royal flush is a hand with a series of cards, all of the same suit ranking ace, king, queen, jack and ten. A straight flush is a five-card sequence where all the cards are of the same suit.

"Full House is a hand comprised of both a three-of-a-kind and a pair. A flush consists of five cards of the same suit. A straight is five cards in sequence, of mixed suits. Three-of-a-kind is three cards of the same rank. Two pair is obvious, two sets of matches. One pair is one match. High card means that it was a really crappy deal and the hand with the highest card wins."

Waiting for her to finish writing down the order, Brody studied her intently. Her brown hair was pulled back and her glasses were perched on her nose, sliding down as she bent over. Still dressed in the clothes she'd worn to work, her body was once again practically covered from head to toe. Not even a hint of cleavage teased him from behind her baggy cream shirt, although for once he was okay with that. The idea of her wearing something seductive at her job didn't sit too well with him. He didn't want any of those perverts looking at her, wanting her the way he did.

Looking up, she picked up her cards and smiled. "Do we ante now?"

"Yes, let's make it a nickel to start," he replied, digging through his change.

They both tossed the money in the center and Brody picked up his cards and looked them over.

"How many cards can we ask for?" Missy asked, studying her hand. She was biting her bottom lip as she concentrated, and Brody had to stop himself from caressing her lip again. It was cute and sexy all at the same time. Kind of like her.

"You can only ask for four cards if you have an ace, if you don't have an ace the maximum is three."

"Okay, I'll take three." Placing her discarded cards to the side, Missy swooped up the new cards Brody sat in front of her.

"Dealer takes three as well," he said, dealing to himself. "Now we bet again."

"Okay, I bet another nickel."

"I see your nickel and raise you a dime." Flipping the coin in, he continued, "Now if you want to continue you have to see my dime. You can see it or you can raise it, it's up to you."

"How many times can I raise?"

"There's generally a limit of three raises a game."

"Well, what do I do if I don't want to raise you, just see your dime?"

"That's 'calling', and you match my raise and then we show each other our hand. If you're in a normal game with five people or more, then it goes around the table, and some people won't raise, they'll fold.

"Let me backtrack." He placed his cards on the table. "You might want to write this down as well."

Missy grabbed her pen and nodded her head for him to continue. "There are five main actions that a player can make when playing poker: bet, call, raise, fold, or check. Bet is to make a wager, call is to see that wager, raise is to up the wager, fold means you give up, and check is the act of not betting anything. If all players check on the same betting round, you still have a chance to win. If someone bets after you check you must call, raise, or fold." Brody ticked off the actions on his fingers. "Are you clear?"

"Yes." She put down her pen and picked up her cards. Looking down at her change, Missy picked up a dime and threw it into the pot. "So I want to call your dime."

"All right, show me what you have."

Laying her cards face up, Missy displayed her hand that had three of a kind. Brody nodded, smiling as he showed her his two pair. Looking up excitedly, Missy said, "I won."

"Yes, you did," he replied proudly. "The pot is yours."

Throwing her arms up in the air, she squealed happily. "I'm the poker queen!"

Laughing, Brody picked up the cards and shuffled again. "The queen, huh? I don't think so, princess."

"Hey, I won, and this is my house, so the house rule is when I win a hand, I am known as the poker queen."

"What happens when I win?"

"Then you're known as the lucky court jester."

"Lucky, huh?"

"Yes," she replied jokingly.

Dealing out the next hand Brody paused. "Poker is a lot like sex. It's ten percent luck, and eighty percent skill."

"What's the other ten percent?"

"Prayer," Brody replied, his face void of all humor.

"You prayed for sex? Somehow I seriously doubt that."

"You should have seen me as a teenager. I prayed so hard for Patty Daniels to let me get to third base. I think it was the second time I had ever prayed so hard in my life."

"What was the first?"

"That I wouldn't come in my pants."

Missy burst out laughing as Brody had hoped she would. Smiling, he watched her face as she tried to get herself back together. "You have the prettiest smile I have ever seen."

Missy stopped laughing and started blushing instead, which caused Brody to laugh. Still red, Missy anted up and picked up her new hand. Giving a quick glance to her notes, she placed two cards on the table and said, "So since you know so much about me, I think it's only fair to know something in return about you."

"Ask away."

"Why don't you just volunteer some information?"

"Because I don't know what you want to hear." Brody dealt their new cards and waited for her to respond. Missy was frowning slightly and he had a feeling that it had nothing to do with her hand and everything to do with him.

"Well, I don't want to pry."

"Missy," he said gently. "You can ask me anything."

"Fine, well, how old are you?"

Laughing Brody replied, "I give you free rein to ask me anything and you ask me that."

"Well, I don't know," she replied, frustrated. "What's your middle name, your favorite color, your IQ, your favorite band, the thing you look for most in a woman, favorite side of the bed, and the last thing you do before you go to bed?"

"Thirty-two, Cameron, blue, I don't know, Metallica, breasts, right, masturbate," he said in one breath, smiling. "And you?"

"Umm, you already know the first two," Missy said. "So let's see, I don't have one, I don't know either, Dave Matthews Band, I don't look for anything in a woman, right, and brush my teeth."

"You don't masturbate?"

"Not before I go to sleep," she replied, her cheeks slightly reddening.

"Why?"

"Can we finish this hand? I'll raise you a nickel."

"Call," he said, throwing in his nickel and laying down his hand at the same time. "I have nothing, you win. So the hand is done, answer the question."

"Why did you call if you didn't have anything?" she asked inquisitively.

Lena Matthews

"It was the easiest way to finish up. So are you going to answer the question?"

"Don't you think that it's a little personal?"

"I told you."

"But I didn't ask you that."

"Fine, it's my turn, so it's my question to you."

"Brody," she groaned, bringing her hands up to cover her face.

Reaching over, he gripped her wrists in his hands and squeezed them slightly before pulling them down to the table. "I love the way you groan my name, but answer the question."

"Let go," she tugged on her wrists.

"Not on your life."

"You're a big bully."

"And you're avoiding the question. I have nowhere to be tomorrow."

"Fine," she huffed. "It's because masturbating is frustrating."

"Why?" Brody replied thickly.

"Because it just leaves me keyed up. It doesn't relax me."

"That would explain your behavior in the office," he said, slowly releasing her wrists. "Was that so hard?"

"Maybe," she pouted, scooping up her change. "Was it so hard to let my wrists go?"

"I got hard the second I touched you, so yeah it was."

She stilled and looked up at him. "I thought we were going to go slow."

"This is my slow mode."

Blanching, she said softly, "That's a scary thought."

"I'm trying here, princess, but you're going to have to meet me halfway."

"My half or your half?"

"Mine," he replied firmly. "I'm more than willing to court you, you deserve it, but taking it slow doesn't mean ignoring my desire for you. You have me on simmer, but the heat is still there. Only it's a constant burning. So, as long as I can't forget I want you, I'm not going to let you forget it."

"That's not slow, Brody."

"It's slow enough." Standing, he reached over the table and brought her to her feet. Brushing his lips against hers, he ached to deepen the kiss, but restrained himself. As hard as he was, Brody knew if she encouraged him, even in the slightest way, nothing short of a miracle would keep him from plunging into her. Pulling back, he said softly, "I think I'll call it a night."

"'Kay," she replied, dazed. Her brown eyes were glazed and her breath shallow.

"Are you free Friday?" Brody asked, releasing her arms and stepping back.

"I think so,"

"Do you want to get together and play again? Say Friday around seven at my place?"

"Sure."

"Great." He smiled, walking to the door; he paused as he opened it. "I had fun."

"So did I," Missy replied, smiling back. Walking to him, she stood on her tiptoes and kissed him quickly on the cheek. "Thanks for coming over."

"My pleasure."

"Do you want me to bring the change on Friday?"

"No," he said, looking down into her eyes. "What we're going to play doesn't require any." Brody walked out the door and closed it behind him before she could utter a sound. Tonight was poker her way... Friday they would play his.

Chapter Five

Missy looked up from the directions Brody had left the day before. Feeling like a schoolgirl, she had kept the message he'd left on her answering machine and had replayed it so many times that it wasn't funny anymore. Just the sound of his voice was enough to send shivers down her spine. She still didn't understand why he was interested in her, but at this point, she no longer cared.

The porch light shined like a beacon in the night on his ranch-style home. The tan-colored house was similar to other homes in the tract-home community, clean and crisp with a well-maintained yard. Parking her car at the curb in front of his house, Missy got out slowly and looked around. This neighborhood was nothing like hers. Nor like the one she grew up in, either.

Her mom had worked two dead-end jobs just to support the two of them her entire life. She died like she had lived, poor and unnoticed, and Missy had wanted a different life for herself. *This kind of life*, she thought as she strolled up his walkway. She doubted Brody knew how lucky he was. Most people in his situation didn't.

Ringing the doorbell, she waited nervously for him to open the door. Heart pounding, she smoothed her hair down and ran her tongue quickly over her front teeth to ensure she didn't have anything stuck in them. Her pulsed quickened as Brody opened the door and smiled down at her. As usual, he looked wonderful. And also as usual, Missy felt completely underdressed. In jean overalls and tight white T-shirt, she had dressed for a casual evening, opting for the comfortable outfit.

Brody, on the other hand, probably thought he looked casual in his khaki Dockers and black form-fitting shirt, but to Missy he looked as if he had stepped off the cover of GQ. Groaning to herself, she wished she could turn back the hands of time and go home to change her clothes. Not that she had anything as nice to wear, but still she wouldn't have gone for the Farmer John look.

"Wow," she said.

Smiling, Brody stepped back to let her enter. "The same goes for you, Ms. Haddan."

"How do you know I wasn't talking about your home?" she teased, stepping into his dimly lit foyer. Looking around, she resisted the impulse to shove her hands deep in her pockets, to prevent herself from breaking anything.

Laughing softly, he replied, "You might be talking about the house, but I'm definitely talking about you."

Rolling her eyes, Missy wrinkled her nose. "Whatever, I look like a reject from *Hee Haw*. I thought we were just playing cards. I feel so underdressed."

"You look great," he said, closing the door. "And I always had a thing for *Hee Haw*." Brody walked closer to her and took her hand, leading her down the hall.

"Besides," he said, leering at her, "overalls are my favorite date clothes."

"Why?"

"Two little snaps and you're nearly undressed. You can't go wrong with that," he teased, leading her into the den. Brody had pulled his navy blue couches to the side and had set up his casino poker table in the middle of the room. There were potato chips and pretzels on the coffee table with a couple of beers chilling in a Corona tin bucket.

Missy turned to him, smiling. She could tell he had gone out of his way to make it feel like a real game for her. "This is amazing," she grinned.

"I wanted it to be as authentic as possible. I even have a football game my brother Bryce taped for me ready in the VCR. A bona fide poker game without the bona fide boneheads."

Beaming, Missy wanted to throw her arms around his neck and kiss him senseless. He was just unreal. Missy looked up at him as he turned and smiled down at her. Throwing caution to the wind, she did just what her body wanted her to do. She reached up and kissed him. Entangling her hands behind his neck, Missy drew him in close and brushed her lips against his.

When she moved back to end the quick peck, Brody stopped her by wrapping his arms around her and saying huskily, "Where do you think you're going?"

Drawing her back in, he kissed her deeply, sliding his tongue between her lips. Missy could feel her body yielding as his tongue probed her parted lips. It had been so long since she had been made love to that her body longed to be consumed.

Ending the kiss, Brody slowly released her and stepped back. "Now that's what I call a thank you kiss."

Missy flushed faintly and avoided his eyes by looking away from his probing stare. "This is wonderful," she gushed.

"I'm glad you like it." Walking to the table, he picked up a remote and aimed it at the bookshelf against the far wall, engulfing the room in soft rock music. "You ready to play?"

"Yes," she said excitedly. Walking to the empty chair, she sat down and began shuffling the cards. "I studied my notes, so I'm ready. Be prepared to lose tons of money." Looking around the table, she said, "Speaking of money, where are the chips?"

"Let's play a couple of warm-up hands first," Brody said, not meeting her eyes.

"Trying to read my signals, are you?" she teased, dealing out the cards.

"That's it." He smiled.

A couple of warm-up hands turned into the best hour Missy had spent in a while. Brody was a complete riot. He kept her laughing and smiling, even making her comfortable enough she forgot to blush, and he'd given her plenty to blush about. Brody's brand of humor leaned towards the blue side, and he never failed to make a suggestive compliment whenever he felt the desire to. He made her feel comfortable and beautiful, but most importantly, he made her feel wanted.

Brody stood up and stretched. His shirt rose a little, teasing her with a quick peek of his midriff. Missy was captivated by the faint trail of dusky hair leading into his pants.

"Want me to take the shirt off so you can get a better look?"

"I wasn't..."

"Liar," he teased. Grabbing the bottom of his shirt, he pulled it over his head. His muscular chest was as defined as Webster's dictionary. Toned and tight, his chest was well developed without being bulgy and his abs were lean and cut. Tossing her the shirt, he winked at her as she fought the need to blush and hide. If he was comfortable being topless, she was going to sit back and enjoy the view.

Brody grabbed two beers out of the tin and brought them back to the table. "So, are you going to leave me at a disadvantage here?" he asked, gesturing to his chest.

"From where I'm sitting, it's not a disadvantage at all."

"Do my ears deceive me, or did you just make a sexual innuendo?"

"Now, would I do that?" Missy batted her eyes mockingly.

"Hell, I'm hoping so," he said, opening the beer. "So, you feeling lucky?"

"Ten percent worth."

"You ready to play for collateral?"

"I brought my money," Missy said, patting her top pocket.

"I don't want your money."

"Are we going to play with chips then?"

"No, not chips."

"Then what?"

"You look good in those overalls, but I'm willing to bet you look better without them."

Her mouth dropped open in shock. "You've got to be kidding."

"I'm completely serious."

"I'm not taking off my pants."

"You only have to take them off if you lose."

"Well, I could lose."

"Then don't."

"Brody..."

"Missy..."

"Look, I know you don't like me saying the F word, but there's no way I'm getting naked if front of you."

"How about something else?"

"What?"

"How about we watch that movie I bought?"

"The porn?"

"Yes."

"So if I lose I have to watch a dirty movie with you, and if I win what do I get?"

"What do you want?"

"Wash my car."

"You could have anything you want, and you want me to wash your car?"

"What's wrong with it?" she asked, irritated. "I told you I suck at this guy/girl thing."

"No, it's fine," he backpedaled. "Okay, if you win I'll wash your car, if I win you watch the movie with me."

"Now, you mean just watch it, right?"

"Yes."

"Nothing funny?"

"I sincerely hope not."

"You know what I mean." Missy frowned.

"I do, and I swear that I won't do anything you don't want me to do."

"That's what I'm afraid of," she mumbled, shuffling the cards. Brody reached over and laid his hand over hers, stopping her.

"What are you afraid of?"

"That we won't just watch the movie."

"I won't force you to do anything you don't want to do, Missy."

"You can't force the willing."

Taking the cards out of her hands, Brody took her hands in his and gently rubbed the back of his thumb against the top of her hand. Looking into her trouble-filled brown eyes, he softened his tone and said sincerely, "Missy, I want you."

"I know."

"Do you want me?"

"I do, but I'm not into casual sex."

"There will be nothing casual about it."

"I don't really know you." She shrugged.

"You know enough."

"Something inside won't let me make this decision."

Standing, Brody pushed the table over and grabbed her up in his arms. "Fine, then I'll make it for you." Quickly capturing her mouth, Brody dominated her lips and her mind.

Pushing her backwards until she was against the wall, he leaned into her and cupped her full, denim-covered breast in his hand while plunging his tongue in her mouth. Missy moaned as he slid his leg between her thighs, pressing his leg up against her moistened mound. Part of her wanted him to stop—a small, tiny, itty-bitty part—but the rest of her was ready to go full steam ahead.

Missy moved back over his leg, riding him and the hard denim seam that was torturing her clit mercilessly. She wondered if she would come from just the pressure of his knee against her, that and the kneading of her breast.

Brody's hand slid up from her breast, to the buckle of her overalls and that was when Missy's red flag started waving in front of her eyes. Dropping her arms from around his shoulders, she caught his hand and stopped him from unbuckling her overalls. Pulling away from her mouth, Brody looked down at her, frustration bleeding out from his eyes.

"Are you saying no?" he demanded, pressing his knee up against her mound.

"No, I'm saying..."

"Are you saying no?"

"No I'm not, but..."

"Shhh," he said, laying his finger against her mouth. Slowly running his finger across her bottom lip, swollen from kissing, he dipped it in her mouth and trailed his moist finger down her mouth to her neck, ending back at her chest.

Brody lowered his leg and took the two clasps that held the overalls together and unclasped them, making the bib fall forward, leaving her chest, covered by her form-fitting white shirt, visible. Missy brought her hands up and covered her chest.

"I'm big," she said helplessly.

Taking her hands off her breasts, Brody pressed one against the bulging crotch of his pants. "So am I."

"But..."

"Here's a new rule," Brody said as he unbuckled the buttons on the side of her overalls. "You are not allowed to say anything else unless it's *'no'* because you want me to stop. Or 'fuck me, Brody, fuck me, right there, yes, yes, yes', or my personal favorite, 'oh my, you're so huge'. Feel free to mix and match them as you please."

"I have a rule too."

"You don't get to make a rule," he teased.

"Yes, I do."

Sighing, he leaned forward and brushed her pouting lips with his. "One rule and one rule only."

"The lights go off."

"Absolutely not."

"No, Brody, I'm serious."

"Me too," he said, stepping back. "I want to see you, Missy, and I want you to see me."

"Well, look at you," Missy said, gesturing towards his chest. "Why wouldn't you want to show that off?"

"And why wouldn't you want to show those off?" he asked, looking at her breasts. "I think you're beautiful, I find you attractive. I'm standing here in front of you hard as hell. What more can I do to make you believe that I want you? All of you."

"I want you too. Just let me have this. I have to work up to this." Missy felt that her heart was breaking. She didn't want to leave without having him, but she wasn't as courageous as he was. It was going to take some time to get used to him, used to him wanting her.

"Damn it," he said, turning away from her. Missy walked up behind him and pressed her breasts to his back. "Missy..."

"Please," she whispered, running her hands over his cool back. Lightly kissing his shoulders, she ran her hands around his sides and to the front, gently scratching down his chest. "Give me this, and I'll let you make another rule."

Brody grabbed her hands and flattened them across his chest, stopping her gentle teasing. "Fine, you get the lights off."

Relief rushed through her and she leaned against him. Brody turned in her embrace and pushed her back slightly so he could look down in her face. "But I get to have you any and every way I want you. You can try to hide in the dark, but before this night is over, I'll know your body by heart."

Chapter Six

Brody wasn't happy at all by the way the evening had turned out. True, he was going to get to have sex with her, but he wanted to do it with the light shining down on her. He wanted to see every single inch of her and taste the parts he couldn't see. Brody wasn't stupid enough to tell her no, so he would just have to settle for loving the fuck out of her and looking another time.

Brody led her back to his bedroom and shut the door behind him. Without turning the light on, he took her to the bed and sat down with her standing between his legs. The bib of her overalls was still undone, leaving her chest in view. Missy's nipples were erect and pointing out of the shirt, and he knew that despite any lingering doubts she might have, she wanted him.

The light in the bathroom, which was left on from when he was getting ready earlier, cast a faint glow in the bedroom. Giving him just enough light to see her, but not enough to satisfy him. Brody drew her close to him and placed his mouth against her shirt, sucking her hard nipple through her clothes. Gripping her ass in his hands, he squeezed her to him as he nibbled on her nipple.

"Brody," she groaned, tugging on his hair. "The light is still on."

Pulling his mouth back, he reluctantly released her nipple and looked up at her with passion-filled eyes. "And we're still clothed. Don't worry, princess, when it comes time to take your clothes off, I'll let you hide behind all the darkness you want."

Pushing her back, he stood up and unbuckled his pants. Sliding them off his hips, he stepped out of them, underwear and all, and stood before her proud and unashamed. "I, on the other hand, have no such qualms about you seeing me naked. I want to know that when you look at me, you desire me." Taking her hand in his, Brody placed it against his hard, aching cock. "Touch me."

Missy drew his cock in her hand and worked it back and forth. Brody gritted his teeth, biting back the need to throw her on the bed and plunge into her. With a slow, steady hand, he tugged her shirt out of her pants and slid his hands underneath it. Cupping her lace-covered breasts, he squeezed them, matching Missy's stroke with squeezes.

"You feel so good," he groaned, leaning his head against hers.

"You too."

Brody released her breasts and moved his hand down to stop hers. Walking away, he went to the bathroom and turned off the light. Turning to her, he said softly, "The lights are off. Get undressed."

Walking back, he sat down in front of her and, with the faint light from the moon, was able to watch her as she undressed. Years spent in special ops had helped him develop good night vision, and he used all the training Uncle Sam had provided him with to look his fill of her lush fullness.

Missy definitely wasn't as large as she thought she was. By fashion-model standards she might have been big, but by his, she was perfect. Her white, creamy thighs were full but toned and she had wide, ample hips. His cock jerked between his legs as he envisioned pounding between her smooth legs.

Pausing before lifting her shirt, Missy gave a soft groan before tugging it over her head. Her softly rounded stomach was framed by her white lace bra and matching panties. He could tell, even in the dark, that she wanted to hide by the way she held her body. When Missy moved her hands behind her back to unclasp her bra, Brody stood up and stopped her, saying, "No, let me."

Brody walked behind her and undid her bra. He took his time sliding his hands up to her shoulders, enjoying the feel of her smooth flesh under his. Her breathing had sped up by the time he pushed the straps down, letting him know in no uncertain terms that she was just as aroused as he. Running his hands down her arms, he moved them across her stomach and up her chest, cupping her heavy mounds in his hands. Her answering moan was enough as he pulled her back against him, rubbing his hard cock against her ass and pinching her nipples between his fingers.

"Some men are ass men, some men are leg men. For me, it's all about the breasts," he whispered in her ear as he played with them.

"Go lay down on the bed," he ordered as he let go of her breasts.

Brody watched as Missy climbed up onto the bed and lay down in the middle. Getting in after her, Brody slid on top of her and moved between her legs. Lifting up on his forearms, he pressed his middle against her moist center and cupped her breasts with his hands. Leaning forward, he pushed her breasts together and tongued her nipples, alternating between them.

Brody circled her areola with his tongue before swooping down and sucking her nipple in his mouth. Pulling on it with his teeth, he nipped the hard nipple as he massaged her other breast, plucking the nipple with his thumb and forefinger.

Missy tangled her hands in his hair, pressing him down harder on her breast. Moaning, she rocked her pelvis up against him, soaking his stomach with her wetness. Brody pulled his mouth away from her wet nipple and said, "Move your hands to the headboard and don't take them away."

"What?" she groaned, looking down at him.

"You heard me," he said, moving up over her body. Getting on his knees, he reached down between them and took his cock in his hand, rubbing the head against her pussy lips. "My way. Remember?"

Whimpering, Missy moved her hands to the headboard and pressed her palms flat against it. Brody moved down her body, pressing kisses to her stomach as he went. Stopping at her belly button, Brody dipped his tongue inside before he moved down to her neatly trimmed mound. Her lips were covered in light brown curly hair that was damp with her dew.

Brody licked her wet slit before opening her lips. Inhaling deeply, he let the scent of her excitement fill his senses. Her essence was spicy and warm, and it beckoned to him, urging him to taste her. Unable to resist, Brody moved his mouth down to her wet heat, drawing circles around her clit with his tongue. He dipped his tongue into her hot center, lapping up her juices.

Missy's moans filled the room as she moved against his tongue. Using his other hand, Brody slid two fingers into her hot pussy, pushing against her walls as he prepared her tight hole for his hard cock. Her moans grew louder as he added a third finger, fucking her with his hand. Sliding his tongue rapidly over her swollen clit, Brody sped up the rhythm of his hand as he felt her body convulsing.

He sucked her clit into his mouth, surrounding the sensitive bud with sucking pressure, until she arched her back and came around his fingers. Drinking up her delicious juices, Brody slipped his fingers out of her shuddering pussy and sheathed his cock with the condom he had laid next to her on the bed.

Taking his cock in his hand, he held her pussy open with his other one and plunged his cock deep inside of her, pausing to let her adjust her body to his size. It was a tight fit, but he knew she would be able to stretch to accommodate his thick member. He would bet, from the tightness of her pussy, it had been a while since she had been with another man. Rocking slowly inside of her, he picked up her leg and wrapped it around his waist so he could control the depth of his entry.

Looking through the darkness into Missy's eyes, Brody said huskily, as he pulled out of her and plunged forward again, "I'm going to fuck you all night."

Lifting her hips, he held them slightly up as he moved in and out of her wet pussy. Her tight walls encircled his length as he pumped in long, full strokes.

Missy's inner walls began to spasm around him. Brody could feel her muscles grasping at his cock repeatedly as she came around him. Throwing her head back, she arched up to him, crying his name as she thrust back against him, powering her motion by pushing herself off the headboard into him.

Biting back his own groan, Brody continued to power into her as he held back his own orgasm. He didn't want this to end so quickly, but it felt like her pussy was trying to squeeze the life out of his cock. Even in the throes of passion, her moist center was still tight, clenching him as she shuddered around him.

"Don't stop. Don't stop," she muttered as she lifted her hands from the headboard and dug her fingers into his ass, pulling him deeper into her.

"I said don't let go," he gritted through clenched teeth.

"Fuck that, fuck me," she begged as she pushed into him.

Jerking out of her, he winced as her nails scratched him in an attempt to keep him inside of her. Sitting back on his haunches, he breathed in deeply, inhaling the scent of their sex in the air. "Turn over," he ordered.

Sitting up, she pushed her sweat-covered hair out of her eyes. "Why?"

"Because I said so."

"Look, I'll just put my hands back up."

Getting on his knees, he pulled her forward and kissed her roughly. He ran his hands down her backside and brought his palm down sharply against her ass cheek. "I told you to roll over."

Missy moved back and rolled over until she was lying on her stomach. Brody bit back a groan as he saw her full, white globes come into view.

"Get up on your knees," he said huskily as he stroked his still erect cock.

"This is not a very dignified position." She chuckled nervously, but she did as he said.

Brody rubbed his cock as she got up on all fours, and moving between her spread legs, bent down and put his fingers in her opening. "Who wants to be dignified?" he moaned as he flicked her clit with his fingers. He held her lips a bit apart so he could slide more easily into her wet body. Pushing the head of his cock in slowly, he eased back into her, giving her a few minutes to once again adjust to the size of his cock, before he started to fuck her.

Gripping Missy's hips, Brody fucked her with a steady rhythmic motion. Her puckered rosette called to him, though. The harder he grasped her thighs, the farther her cheeks spread, the more the need to fuck her delectable ass grew inside him. He wanted to slide his cock inside her forbidden hole. Pulling out slowly, he rubbed his hand around his condom-covered cock and lubed his fingers with her juices.

Brody continued his steady rhythm as he ran his wet finger over her puckered hole. Fleetingly over the rim, not yet pushing in, but moistening it.

Missy tensed and looked over her shoulder at him. "Are you going to..."

Gripping her hips again, Brody replied, "Would you let me?"

"Umm," she said. Trying to talk while being fucked wasn't something she was obviously good at. "I've never done it before."

Brody slid his cock out until only the tip remained in. As he plunged back in, he leaned forward and pulled her up off the bed. He cupped her breasts, teasing and tugging on her nipples as he gyrated his hips up into Missy. "That wasn't a no," he groaned.

"It's your way, Brody," she moaned, gushing down on him as she rocked into his cock. "Anything you want, anywhere."

Her words sent chills down his spine. Brody released her breasts so he could grip her hips as he powered into her, speeding up his rhythm. Brody fucked her like tomorrow would never come.

His cock, hard and thick, plunged into her over and over until he felt her body began to shake. The walls of her pussy once again clenched down on him as her body neared release. Unbeknownst to Missy, she had just hit on his sexual Achilles heel. Brody craved to make her body his, completely.

He had this caveman urge to dominate her sexually, none of that S and M shit, just to be able to do anything and everything sexually satisfying to her that he could. For Missy to say what she said, and not know what he wanted, drove him mad, because despite what she said here in the heat of passion, she wouldn't mean it later. And he had to fuck that thought out of his head. She should be his, all his.

Moaning, Missy shook and screamed his name as she came again. Shoving her ass back at him, she pounded him as much as he had pounded her. The sounds of her satisfaction rocked him to his core and tore the orgasm out of him. Literally causing him to cry out, part in pleasure and part in pain, as he shoved into her for one last stroke, gripping her harder than he had all evening. Brody roared his release like a cry to heaven. The feel of her body, the thought of having ownership of her body, had been too much for him to handle.

Looking down at Missy, who was still on her knees, but laying forward flat, he watched as her body quaked with orgasmic aftermaths, and heard her lightly chant "Oh My God" over and over again.

Brody pulled out of her body slowly and sat back on his butt. His limp cock lay tired and wet between his quivering thighs, shaken from the Olympic pole-vaulting it had just supported. Aching and wet, his body felt alive for the first time in years.

Moving to the edge of the bed, he looked at Missy, who still had her ass up in the air. "You okay, sweetheart?" he asked, rubbing her back.

"I'm better than okay." She smiled, turning her head. "Can I move yet, or do I have to still lie this way?"

Chuckling, Brody lovingly brushed stray hairs away from her face. "You can move. If you can."

Missy chuckled herself and slowly stretched her legs out from under her. "I'm not so sure I can move far."

"Don't, I'll take care of you." Brody got up from the bed, walked to the connecting bathroom and turned on the light. He grabbed a washcloth off the rack, first cleaning himself and disposing of the well-used condom, and then got a fresh towel out and wet it with warm soapy water for Missy.

Brody walked back towards the bed and turned on the nightstand lamp. He looked down on a lightly sleeping Missy and smiled. She was still lying on her stomach, leaving her delectable derrière exposed to his watchful eye. Cursing the manners his mother had crammed down his throat, he turned off the light before cleaning between her legs. Brody knew that if she woke up in the midst of him tidying her up and saw the light, she would kill him, and things were going way too good to screw them up now for a quick peek. The last thing he wanted to do was to give Missy any reason to think he was untrustworthy.

Taking the towel back to the bathroom, he dropped it into the sink and turned off the light. He wanted to shower, but he didn't want to chance her disappearing while he was cleaning up, so a whore's bath would have to do, he thought, disgruntled.

Climbing back on the bed with her, he slid next to her, gathered the folded sheet at the bottom, and pulled it up over them. Spooning her from behind, he thought back over their little fuck fest.

Missy had been as delicious as he had always imagined. She had taken every stroke and given back two. She was spectacular, and she was his. Brody knew that she would be a challenge, even after all this, but he was up for the task. The only problem would be with him being able to keep tight control of his domineering desires.

Chapter Seven

Missy awoke to the smell of frying bacon drifting in the air. Opening her eyes, she glanced around the room trying to get her bearings. This was not her apartment, she thought, sitting up, startled in the strange bed. The covers fell off her sore, naked body, and that quickly she remembered where she was and whom she had been with.

Smiling, she lay back in the comfortable bed and wiggled under the covers. Her body felt deliciously sore. She tingled from head to toe, and ached in places she hadn't since riding her friend's horse in the seventh grade. Life was good, she thought with a smile.

Looking over at the nightstand, Missy spied her glasses, leaned over and picked them up. Plopping them on, she looked around the room, something she wasn't able to do last night due to the lack of light. Brody's bedroom was Asian inspired, with few furnishings and lots of wide, empty space. She glanced at the clock on the nightstand and sighed in relief that she still had several hours before she had to be at work.

Missy hopped out of bed and picked up the robe lying over the foot of the black silk bedspread. The door opened as she tied the belt loosely around her waist. Turning, she looked into the eyes of a smiling Brody, who was holding a cup of coffee.

"Morning, sleepyhead," he said, coming into the room. Dropping a quick kiss on her lips, Brody grinned as he handed Missy the mug. "I didn't know if you had to work today. I was about to come and wake you up."

"Not until two," she said, sipping the black coffee. "What about you?"

"My brother and I are getting together later today."

"Well, I'll just get out of your way," Missy replied, setting the cup down on the nightstand and walking towards his bathroom.

"Whoa there, Trigger." Brody laughed, pulling on the robe. "Who said you were in my way? We have plenty of time for breakfast."

Smiling, Missy felt relieved. She didn't want him to think that she was trying to crowd him. There was nothing she wanted to do more than to linger with him over coffee and toast, and talk about their day. Brody was very habit forming and like all bad habits, he would be hell to give up.

"Let me just hop in the shower and I'll meet you in the kitchen."

"You have five minutes. After that I won't be able to vouch for breakfast."

"I'll be there in four," she teased, going into the bathroom. Turning on the shower, Missy let it warm up as she stared at herself in his mirror. Her brown hair was matted and flat on one side, and the little trace of makeup she had applied had long since disappeared. She looked like hell, but she couldn't help smiling.

Last night had been one of the most amazing nights of her life. Brody was an incredible lover. He had played her body like a fine instrument. Missy hadn't come that hard and that often ever. He had demanded and she had surrendered; it was the hottest thing she had ever done. It was amazing how much power he had over her. Missy knew that she would do any and everything he wanted, no questions asked, and that was a scary thought.

Stepping into the shower, she let the hot water soak her tender muscles. Leaning back, she wet her hair and washed it with the shampoo on the ledge. She didn't want to keep him waiting, but she wanted to be able to look at least halfway presentable when she sat across from him at the table.

Missy rinsed off and stepped out of the shower. Wrapping the soft cotton towel around her, she walked into the bedroom, and saw her purse sitting on the bed. Opening it, she took out her comb and untangled her long hair. Pulling out the spare clip she kept in her bag, she clipped her hair up, allowing a few strands to fall down and curl around her face.

Missy looked around for her clothes but couldn't see them. She knew that she had left them on the floor, but they were gone now. Putting the robe back on, she left his room and followed her nose to the kitchen.

Brody was dressed only in jeans and was sitting at the round table drinking coffee and reading the paper. He looked comfortable and absolutely irresistible. He had set the table for two, with a glass of juice and a cup of steaming coffee in front of her plate. Brody had also taken the time to add a fresh cut rose across her empty plate. It was sweet and romantic, and completely not what she was used to.

"Do you know where my clothes are?" Missy asked, sitting across from him at the table. Picking up the flower, she inhaled its powerful scent before setting it down next to her plate.

"Yes," he said, standing up and walking to the stove. Brody placed the newspaper down on the kitchen counter and opened the oven, removing two hot plates loaded with pancakes, eggs and bacon. Setting them in the center of the table, he speared three pancakes and placed them on his plate.

Waiting expectantly, Missy watched as he filled his plate. "Well, where are they?"

"I've hidden them." He grinned, taking a bite off his bacon.

"Why?" she asked, confused.

"Because I wanted to eat breakfast with you dressed in nothing but my robe." Brody wiggled his brows in jest, forcing a laugh from Missy.

"All you had to do was ask."

"Better safe than sorry."

"You're deranged."

"So I've heard." Pointing his fork at her empty plate, Brody asked, "Are you going to eat, or just decorate the place?"

Missy rolled her eyes and reached for a pancake. She was a little apprehensive about eating in front of him, but she knew that if she didn't at least have something he would make a big deal out of it.

Eyeing her plate, he frowned, "Aren't you hungry?"

"No," she lied. She was actually famished, but she would die a slow, agonizing death before admitting that to him. "I'll grab something later."

"Just take a little more." He forked another pancake onto her plate. "You'll need your energy later."

Flushing, she cut into her pancakes and ignored the soft chuckle coming from him. Taking a bite, she groaned in delight at the warm, syrupy flavor. Missy hadn't had pancakes in ages, and they tasted divine. Looking up, she noticed that Brody was no longer eating, just staring at her hungrily.

"What's wrong?" she asked, wiping at her chin. "Do I have syrup everywhere?"

"Make that noise again," he said huskily.

"What noise?"

"That little moan thing you did."

"Why?"

"Because it's exactly how you sounded last night."

"Brody." Missy could feel the heat spreading over her flushed skin.

"What was the best part for you last night?" Brody asked, his tone heavy with arousal.

"I loved everything."

"Did one thing stand out?"

"It was all mind-blowing," Missy smiled shyly. "What about for you? What did you like?"

Brody shifted slightly, and if Missy hadn't been watching him so closely, she might have missed it. Something inside of her froze. Was he regretting last night? Did she do something or not do something that he wanted?

"I loved it all too." Brody smiled, but it didn't quite reach his eyes.

"What's wrong?" Missy put down her fork and tried to catch his eyes. "Did I do something wrong?"

Reaching across the table, Brody took her hand in his and said. "Of course not, you were wonderful, are wonderful."

"Then why all the questions?"

Gripping her hand tighter, Brody seemed apprehensive about something. Butterflies rumbled in her stomach. "Tell me," she implored.

"What would you say if I asked you to give me head?"

"You want me to blow you?"

"No," he smiled slightly. "Well, sort of, but would you do it?"

"Yes."

"Would you let me tie you up?"

"Do you want to?"

"What I want is to know how far would you be willing to go?"

"For what?"

"To please me."

Taken aback, Missy looked at him, confused. "Well, how far would you be willing to go?" she asked defensively.

Looking into her eyes, Brody held her gaze and said with conviction, "I'd be willing to do anything for you. If it got you hot, made you wet, turned you on, I would do it in a second."

Eyes widening, Missy felt her stomach drop. Her nipples hardened and brushed against the cotton of her robe. She felt the certain urge to cross her legs, to prevent the moisture she knew was building from escaping from her now-throbbing pussy.

Brody looked down at the robe and eyed her erect nipples. "I see the thought of me doing anything for you is having the same effect as the thought of you doing it for me."

"What do you want from me, Brody?"

"Simply put, Missy, I want total and complete control over your body."

Missy's mouth dropped open in shock. Never had such simple words had such an arousing effect on her.

"What do I get out of it?" she asked. She was surprised that her voice was so steady, when inside she was a mass of quivering nerves.

"Mind-blowing orgasms, for starters."

"Well, I had that last night, and you didn't control me."

"Didn't I?" he asked, arching his brow.

"What else?" Missy ignored his arrogant comment. Although he was right, she didn't need to be reminded of it.

"What else do you want?"

"I want the same control over you," Missy quickly added before he could say anything. "Not all the time, but if I want you to do something, you have to do it."

"Deal," he said, pushing back from the table. "Can I go first?"

"Yes," Missy said, wetting her lips.

"I want your mouth on me." Brody undid his pants and pulled out his semi-erect cock.

Missy stood and walked over to him. Dropping to her knees in front of him, she took his cock in her hand. She looked down at his growing erection hungrily. Missy's pussy ached to have him in her. Leaning forward, she licked the head, tasting his pre-cum as it seeped out of his slit. He tasted salty, masculine and she couldn't wait to have him coming in her mouth.

Spreading the slick coating around his shaft, she stroked her hand down on him as she leaned over and took him in her mouth. Brody let out a deep masculine groan as she swallowed the length of him. She worked her lips back up his thick cock, and tongued the head before dropping back down on him again. With a motion older than time, Missy licked and sucked him, all the while gripping his shaft, milking him with her hand.

With her free hand she reached down to cup his balls. She massaged them as she ran her tongue around the eye of his hard cock.

Brody groaned and uttered through clenched teeth, "That's it, baby, suck me." Reaching down, he slid his hands inside of the loosened robe and tugged on her breasts, freeing them from the clothing. Taking her nipples in his fingers, he pinched and tweaked them, forcing a groan from deep inside her throat.

"Touch yourself," he ordered, and Missy obeyed. Releasing his balls, she slid her hand to her breast and tried to touch her nipples. "No, baby, your pussy. Touch that sweet pussy for me."

Missy had never masturbated in front of anyone in her life. Slipping her hand between her thighs, she slid her busy fingers over her wet slit and pressed against her hard clit. Rubbing her clit and blowing him at the same time wasn't easy. It took a lot of coordination, but by the time she had him near orgasm, she too was riding the edge.

His moans got louder as he pushed his cock up into her mouth. Releasing one of her breasts, he slid his hand behind her neck into the back of her hair. Gripping her hair through the clip, he fucked her face as she deep-throated his cock. Missy's nimble fingers slid inside her pussy as she fucked herself and rubbed her clit with her thumb.

"Brody, where are you?" a masculine voice called from down the hall.

Missy started to stop, but Brody's firm pressure at the back of her head urged her on. "Don't stop, baby, keep sucking me."

"Hey, Brody," the voice called, getting closer to the kitchen.

Missy ignored all sense of decorum and tightened her mouth around his cock as she jerked his cock faster. Moving her hand in the same rhythm, she reached her release seconds before he came, filling her mouth with his warm salty fluid.

"Hey, bro, there you..."

Missy was too busy swallowing to look up, not that she would have if she were done. She was too embarrassed and aroused to remember Emily Post's rules for meeting your boyfriend's family while you had a mouth full of semen.

"I, umm..." said the man, "I'll be in the other room."

Brody chuckled harshly as he tried to slow down his breathing. He took his softening penis from her mouth and looked down at her with adoration in his eyes.

"That was fucking wonderful," he said, placing her wet fingers into his mouth. He licked up her juices one finger at a time, then pulled her up until she was sitting on his lap.

"You were unbelievable," he whispered, kissing her softly on the lips. "Did you get to come?"

"Yes," she said, glancing at the open door. "Who was that?"

"My brother," Brody cradled her breasts in his hands and lovingly caressed her. Bending forward, he took her nipple in his mouth and molded it with his lips.

"Umm, Brody," she pulled back. "Your brother is in the other room."

"Probably wishing he was in my shoes right now." He chuckled, sliding his hand between her thighs.

"No." She tried to close her legs. "You have company."

"Let him find his own girl." Missy groaned deeply as Brody slipped his fingers inside of her moist opening and quickly brought her back to the edge. Keeping her eyes on the door, she arched into him as he sucked her breast and finger-fucked her at his table. This was the most enjoyable breakfast she had ever had, she thought as she came, biting back a moan.

Chapter Eight

Brody was having a hard time getting Missy to agree to come out of the bedroom. After their little rendezvous was interrupted, she had insisted on him giving her back her clothes. He didn't see what the big deal was. The robe covered her completely, but she was very adamant about it. He took her clothes out of his closet, where he had placed them this morning, and watched as she quickly dressed. The only good thing about her embarrassment was she forgot about not wanting him to see her naked in her haste to put her clothes on.

"I have no idea how long he's going to be here, and you have to be to work in two hours, so you're going to have to come out of here eventually," he said as patiently as he could.

"Then take him to another room so I can leave."

Sighing, Brody rolled his eyes. "Missy, he's my brother. You're going to have to meet him sometime."

"It doesn't have to be now, with the smell of your semen fresh on my breath."

"You can borrow my toothbrush, for Christ's sake," he muttered.

"Brody, either you make him leave or I'm staying in here until doomsday."

"What are you so embarrassed about? It was my cock hanging out."

"Yes, but it was my mouth around your cock. And it was my hand between my thighs, and my breasts your hands were squeezing. What the hell is he going to think?"

"He's going to think I'm the luckiest son of a bitch in the world. Now snap out of it and come say hi."

"No," she said firmly, crossing her arms over her chest.

"You are just being stubborn."

"And your point is…"

"Arrg," he fumed, storming out of the bedroom. Of all the hardheaded, stubborn women in the world, he had to end up with their queen. Walking into his living room, he scowled at Bryce, who was kicking back on the couch with a magazine in his lap.

"It's about time," Bryce joked, throwing the magazine on the couch. Standing up, he walked over to Brody and gave him a quick hug, pounding him on his still-bare back. "I thought you'd gone back for seconds."

Pushing him away, Brody resisted the urge to knock him on his ass. "Don't you know how to knock?"

"I did," Bryce grinned, good-naturedly. "But apparently you were too occupied to hear."

"Which should have told you something."

"Hey, you could have stopped at any time. You had to hear me calling you."

"Did it look like I was in any place to pause for station identification?"

Roaring with laughter, Bryce dropped back down onto the couch, holding his sides in merriment.

"Would you shut up?" Brody demanded, looking over his shoulder for any sign of Missy. If she heard Bryce laughing, she would never come out.

"I'm sorry, man, but you're killing me."

"No, I'm not, but I'm about to."

That only seemed to spur Bryce on. Brody's scowl only seemed to make Bryce laugh harder. "If you don't shut the hell up, I'm going to pull your bottom lip over your head."

Chuckling, Bryce pulled himself back together, still grinning like a fool. "So what did you do with your gal?"

"She's in the bedroom."

"What? She too tired to come out and say hi?"

"Not too tired, too embarrassed."

"Embarrassed?" Bryce questioned. "Why?"

"Why do you think, dummy?"

"Ahh, she doesn't have to be embarrassed. Now I feel bad."

"As well you should," Brody said, plopping onto the couch next to him. Pulling the magazine from under his ass, he threw it at Bryce, smacking him in the head.

Feeling a little bit better when Bryce said ouch, he sat back and looked at him.

"Should I go apologize?"

"I don't know," Brody shrugged. "She says she's not going to come out until you leave."

"Does she know that I have no life and no place to go?" He grinned.

"No." He grinned back. "But I guess she's about to find out."

Bryce shook his head and he began to fill Brody in on the new improvement he had made to his shop. Bryce was a mechanic and he had just bought a little shop he was fixing up so he could open his own business. Brody was happy his little brother had finally found something he enjoyed.

Bryce, unlike Brody, had never excelled in school. He had been fifteen when he was diagnosed with dyslexia, too late to really do him any good. Bryce had used it as an excuse to drop out of school and had only recently, with Brody's help, received his GED. It was something Brody was very proud of, but on the same hand, something Bryce didn't like to talk about.

They had been talking for fifteen minutes when Brody heard his bedroom door open. Missy sheepishly walked into the room, her purse on her arm, aiming for a quick getaway. But Brody wasn't having any of that. Jumping up, he took her arm and proudly introduced her to a smiling Bryce.

"Bryce, I'd like you to meet the apple of my eye, Missy. Missy, my no-knocking brother, Bryce."

Reddening, Missy put up a brave front and held her hand out to him. Smiling shyly, she shook Bryce's hand and tried to no avail to pull it back. Bryce, much like Brody, wasn't about to let her slink away.

"I was wondering how long you were going to stay in there," Bryce teased lightly, pulling her down next to him on the couch. Brody sat down on the loveseat and smiled as his brother tried to charm Missy.

"Well, truth be told," she smiled. "If I could have fit out the window, I would have been long gone."

"That sounds like you are trying to make a fat comment to me," warned Brody.

Missy stuck out her tongue at him, making Bryce grin. "All I was saying was…"

"I know what you were saying, and you heard what I said too."

"Am I missing something?" inquired a confused Bryce.

"Your brother is under the mistaken impression he can tell me what to do."

"I thought you agreed I could," Brody said, raising a brow mockingly at her. Missy's eyes widened, and if looks could kill, Brody would have been days dead. Chuckling to himself, he knew he would pay for that later. Hoping to change the subject, he said, "Missy's under the mistaken impression that she's fat."

"You have to be kidding me," said Bryce, looking Missy over. "What, you're a size sixteen, eighteen at the most?"

Missy's mouth dropped open in shock. "I can't believe you just said that."

"What?" questioned Bryce.

"You have to forgive him, sweetheart," Brody said, smiling over at her. "Bryce was raised by wolves."

"What?" Bryce asked again. "You're perfect the way you are. I'm sure Brody has told you that more times than you can count."

"What, are you a chubby-chaser too?" she asked teasingly.

Both men instantly quieted. Brody knew how Bryce felt about that term. The same way he did, insulted. Brody slowly counted to ten, trying to rein in his temper. He was damn tired of Missy making backhanded comments about her weight, and even more tired of her questioning his desire for her. He was attracted to her. Not because she was thick and curvy in all the right places, but because she had a way about her. And he was going to teach her that, if it was the last thing he did.

"What?" Now it was Missy's turn to be confused.

"You had to go over that line, didn't you?" Brody asked quietly.

"What did I say?"

"Not only is that an insulting thing to say about me, it's an insulting thing to say about yourself."

"That I'm chub—" Missy stopped in the middle of her sentence, finally catching on to what she was saying.

"I warned you about that," Brody said, standing.

Missy gulped and pushed back in the couch. "I was only kidding, Brody."

"I'm not." He pulled her up from the couch. Missy tried to jerk away, but he held on tighter. Brody sat down on the couch and pulled her over his lap.

"Brody, don't," she wailed, kicking her feet, barely missing Bryce, who stood as Brody sat down. "I was just kidding. Bryce, help me."

"I think if I'm going to help anyone, it's going to be him. You need any help, big brother?"

"Not yet, but she is a bit feisty." Brody brought his palm down sharply on her ass.

"I'd be more than willing to hold her arms for you," Bryce said huskily. Brody looked up, surprised, into his brother's aroused eyes. He had known for years they had the same taste in women, so he should have figured they would also have the same taste in pleasure.

Brody paused in between smacks to rub Missy's ass. He knew his own strength and could tell from her yelps he wasn't hurting her. Of the two of them, he was the only one who was hurting. From the moment he had taken her over his lap he had gotten hard, and from the look in his brother's eyes, he wasn't the only one.

"Do you hear that, princess? Bryce is offering to help," he said as he gently rubbed her ass. "Do you want him to hold your hands while I tend to your ass?"

Missy froze and looked up at Bryce. Brody could tell that she was embarrassed to be in this position, but more embarrassed Bryce had asked to help. He let her go, and she dove back on the couch and buried her ass in the cushion.

"You people are twisted," she grumbled.

"We're twisted," Brody countered, looking over at his brother. They were both aroused because he had spanked her, so maybe they were a little twisted. "You're the one who keeps saying things so I will spank you."

"I do not," she denied, blushing. "You just don't like to hear the truth."

"Whose truth, Missy?" Brody could feel himself getting angry all over again.

"Everyone's, Brody."

"Not everyone's. Let me..."

"Hey, I think this is where I head out," Bryce said, holding up his hands. His eyes had lost the aroused edge to them and now simmered again with amusement.

"You don't have to go," Missy said, standing. "I need to be leaving anyway."

"Why?" asked Brody.

"Because I have to go home and get ready for work."

"Sounds to me like you're trying to run."

"Sounds to me like she'd be smart to," Bryce said.

Missy and Brody both turned and glared at Bryce, which made him chuckle. Shaking her head and muttering something about men, Missy picked up her discarded purse and swung it over her shoulder.

"It was nice meeting you," she said to Bryce. Turning to Brody, she leaned down and kissed him softly on the lips. "I'll talk to you later."

"Let's get together tonight."

"Can't. I have plans."

"Plans?"

"Yes, you know those things you make when you intend to do something."

"With who?" he inquired.

"Scott."

"Scott!" Brody practically roared his name. "What are you doing with him?"

"Stuff," she hedged, frowning. "I'll call you later, okay?"

"Fine," he bit out.

Watching her leave, Brody sat stiffly on the couch, resisting the urge to grab her and force her to tell him what she was doing. He wasn't normally this possessive with women, but with Missy, it was an entirely different story.

"Uh oh," Bryce said, sitting down on the couch next to him. "That's not a happy look."

"Fuck off, Bryce."

"Who's this Scott guy? An ex-boyfriend?"

"No, just a friend."

"If he's just a friend, why did the sound of his name make you want to kill?"

"I don't like him."

"Why?"

"Because he's spending time with Missy," Brody admitted.

"What, you can't share her?" teased Bryce.

"If I'm not willing to share her with you, what makes you think I'd share her with some little prick?"

"What do you mean?" Bryce asked, his smile dropping from his face.

"Oh please, I'm not blind."

"I would never make a move on your girl."

"Of course you wouldn't, but if I asked you to join us, you would say..."

"No," Bryce lied weakly. Brody chuckled at the sheepish look on his brother's face. "Well, I would think no for a second."

"Then it's probably a good thing I don't ask," Brody teased.

"Good for you maybe," Bryce grumbled.

Chuckling, Brody felt his mood lightening. Bryce always had that affect on him. His brother was easygoing by nature, and hardly ever got mad. He was the level one in the family, and Brody's best friend.

"So you want to do something tonight?" asked Bryce

"I already have plans."

"Doing what?"

"Stalking my girlfriend and a prick named Scott," Brody said jokingly—well, sorta joking, he thought. Looking over at his brother, he asked, "You want to come?"

"I wouldn't miss it for the world," Bryce answered.

Chapter Nine

It was going to be a long, sucky night, Missy thought, scrubbing the spreading spot on the carpet. Not only did every pervert in the world stop by Harris's today, they all decided she was an easy mark. Missy wondered if they could just look at her and see she had just been laid, or if there was a lasting aroma that mounds of soap and mouthwash couldn't erase. It seemed as if everyone was giving her knowing looks and lewd come-ons. And Scott, well, he had just straight up lost his mind.

He had come to her apartment tonight so she could help him fill out the form for her friend Kayla's new toy. Kayla had invented an anal stimulator, also known as The Walnut Wand, a sex toy for men, and Scott was one of her test subjects. Missy had introduced them, she knew Kayla needed men to try it out and she knew Scott was looking for part-time work. It seemed to be a perfect partnership, until tonight.

Scott had told her several days ago at school that his roommate was having people over and wanted to know if it would be okay for him to use her spare room to do the latest test. Missy hadn't seen anything wrong with it, he would go in the room by himself, handle his business, and then they could do the survey. It sounded simple, but boy, had she been wrong.

While they had been sitting on the couch, looking over the survey, Scott had actually made a move on her. He bent over and tried to kiss her. Shocked, Missy had pushed him away and accidentally spilled her grape juice all over him, her couch and the floor. Scott was now in the bathroom cleaning up as she scrubbed the floor. Missy had absolutely no idea how to deal with him hitting on her. She was confused, weirded out and totally unable to figure out how to put things back to normal. Even if she and Brody hadn't gotten together, she would have said no to Scott. He was her friend and that's all he would ever be.

Brody would... Groaning, she stood up and walked over to the trash. Brody would blow a gasket if he knew what Scott had tried to do. Missy could already tell he had a problem with Scott and her just being friends, which was tough titties for him, because she wasn't going to stop being Scott's friend, unless they couldn't resolve this little issue.

Sighing, Missy jumped as she heard the pounding on her door. Walking to the door, she peered apprehensively through the peephole. Moaning, she grimaced and muttered, "Just what I need," as she saw Brody's distorted image in the hole. There was no way in hell this was going to end well.

"What are you doing here?" she asked when she opened the door.

"That doesn't sound like happiness to see me," Brody said, pushing past her into the room. Bryce stood in the doorway, smiling sheepishly as he shrugged his shoulders. Missy rolled her eyes and gestured for him to follow his lunatic of a brother in.

"I'm happy, just confused," Missy said, buying herself some time. Everything would be fine if Scott came out of the bathroom dressed.

"We were in the neighborhood," said Brody, looking down her hall.

"Liar." Crossing her arms, she said, "I have company, Brody."

"Yeah?" he asked, crossing his arms mimicking her. "Where is he?"

"He's in the bathroom." Biting her lip, Missy tried to decide if she should tell him about what had happened. If she didn't tell him and he by chance found out some other way, he was going to be really pissed off. "I have to talk to you about something."

"What?" he scowled.

"Don't mind me, folks." Bryce made himself comfortable on her couch. "Just pretend that I'm not here. I know I'm trying to."

They both turned and frowned at him. "Not now or anything, but later okay?"

"I don't think so." Brody scowled.

"Look, Scott is here and something kind of happened," Missy hedged, not quite meeting his eyes. This was going to be bad. So very, very bad. "But let me get rid of him and we can talk about it in the bedroom."

"Why do you have to get rid of him first?" Brody demanded, his eyes hardening as his body tensed.

"Hey, Missy, do you see where I put my..." Scott said, coming out of her bathroom, dressed in jeans and nothing else. He was holding his shirt in one hand, and his pants were partially undone.

"Oh shit!" Bryce said, jumping up.

"What the fuck is this?" Brody yelled. Moving forward towards Scott, Brody uncrossed his arms, brought them to his sides and curled his clenched hands into fists.

Missy frantically moved in front of Brody, stopping him from getting to Scott. "Brody, calm down," she said, throwing herself against him.

"Fuck that!" he said, moving her out of the way. Missy grabbed him from behind, pulling on him, and let out a loud screech as she was picked up by Bryce and held away from Scott.

"Bryce, let me go."

"I will, sugar." Bryce said, pulling her closer to him. "Just as soon as he beats the piss out of your friend."

"Hey, man, it's not what you think," Scott denied, holding his hands up in front of him. "Nothing happened."

"Sure, I believe you." Brody pushed him back against the wall and shoved his knee into his groin. "And I'm going to make sure that nothing ever happens again."

"Brody, stop it this instant," Missy screamed. Pulling her arm back, she elbowed Bryce in the stomach with all her might. Surprised, Bryce released her as he grabbed his stomach. Seizing the moment, Missy pushed away from him and charged Brody, jumping on his back. Brody let out a big "Ouuuff" as she pulled back on him, forcing him to release Scott, who slumped on the floor in relief.

"Stop it, you big idiot." Yanking on his neck, she hung on for dear life.

Brody stepped away from Scott and wrapped his hands around her arms, trying to free his neck. "Bryce, come and get her off of me."

Bryce stood up, still holding his stomach, and pulled on Missy, who had her legs and her arms wrapped around Brody. Scott, seeing his chance for escape, stood up and raced past the wrestling trio and into the hall. The slamming of the door was like water thrown on a screeching cat. Everyone froze. The apartment was as silent as a grave, except for the sound of the heavy breathing rasping out of their chests.

"Get off of me," Brody demanded, giving Missy's arms one final tug.

Missy slid off his back and fell into the arms of Bryce, who was rubbing his stomach softly.

Turning to his brother, Brody fumed, "I thought I told you to take care of her. Now look what you did. You let that prick get away."

"Look what I did?" Bryce shouted back, stunned. "What about what you did? You're supposed to be a badass special-ops everybody-kung-fu-fighting-motherfucker, yet you couldn't get one small girl off your back."

"I didn't see you doing a good job of it either."

"I didn't enlist in the Marines, fucker. I got high and hung out on the corner."

"I could tell by the way you fight."

Missy couldn't believe her ears. They had gone from trying to fight Scott to fighting each other. They were crazy. "Heckle! Jeckle!" she yelled, drawing both of their eyes to her. "Will you two shut up?"

Pushing past Bryce, Missy forced her way out of the hall and dropped down on the couch, close to tears. Scott was never going to talk to her again. Kayla either, once she got wind that Scott hadn't filled out the survey.

"Oh no," Brody warned, pissed off. "You don't get to cry. You didn't just walk in on some half-dressed woman coming out of my bathroom."

"Nothing happened, Brody."

"That's not what it looked like to me."

"That's because you're a stubborn jackass who doesn't listen to anyone."

"She's got you there, bro. You do have several jackass-like qualities."

"Shut up, Bryce," Brody threw over his shoulder. "Do you really expect me to believe that nothing happened between you and the half-ass-naked man?"

"Yes!" she shouted.

"Now which one of us is being a jackass?"

"Look, Scott and I weren't doing anything."

"Then why was he coming out of your bathroom half-naked?"

"There's a perfectly good explanation for that."

"I'm waiting."

"Give me a minute," Missy said, thinking of the best way to explain the situation. "It's a really long story."

"I've got time."

"Fine," she muttered, running her hands through her hair. "It's complicated. And long. Very, very long."

"Then fucking Cliff Note it for me," shouted Brody, pacing in front of her.

"Kayla, the girl from the store who I was talking with that night you came in." She continued when Brody nodded his head. "Well, she needed a few test subjects for a sex toy she's making and I introduced Scott to her. I knew he needed some extra money for books and stuff, and she had said she would pay per study, so I talked to Scott and…"

"I thought this was the fucking Cliff Notes," he spewed.

"Fine," Missy shouted. Taking a big breath, she said as quickly as possible. "I've been helping Scott with the research, and tonight he came over to work on it."

"Helping him how?" Brody asked quietly.

"Well, it's a sex toy…"

"You fucked that pencil neck."

"No," she gasped. "I've never, ever had sex with him."

"Then what did you mean?"

"I mean I was helping him fill out the survey and stuff. But today he came over and asked if he could do the research here."

"What kind of research?" Brody's eyes narrowed.

"Well, he had to use the anal stimulator on himself and..."

"You mean he fucked himself in the ass?" Bryce questioned amusedly.

"Shut up, Bryce," Missy yelled.

"Let me get this straight. Your boy Scott fucked himself with this anal thing while you what, took notes?"

"Of course not. I was supposed to wait until he was done and then we were going to do the survey."

"But..."

"But he kind of kissed me."

"What the fuck?" Brody yelled. "You let that son of a bitch kiss you?"

"I didn't say I let him."

"So then he forced himself on you?"

"No," Missy denied. She didn't want Brody to get the wrong idea. "Scott didn't do anything wrong, not force wrong anyway. He just hit on me, that's it."

"I wonder why he thought he could?"

Missy didn't like the tone of his voice. Standing up she faced him with her hands on her hips. "What is that supposed to mean?"

"You tell him it's okay for him to come over here and fuck himself in your room and you wonder how he got the wrong idea."

Gasping, Missy couldn't believe her ears. "So wait a minute, now it's my fault?"

"Did you really think he was just coming over here to play with a toy?"

"Yes."

"You are so fucking naïve."

"Maybe you're so fucking cynical."

"Cynical! Cynical!"

Bryce stood up and tried to intervene. "Maybe if the two of you..."

"Shut up, Bryce." Missy and Brody both turned and yelled at him.

"I'm not going to take too many more 'shut up, Bryces' from you two," Bryce said angrily.

Ignoring him, Missy and Brody turned back to each other. Brody's nostrils were flared, and Missy could tell that he was having a hard time keeping what little was left of his temper under wraps. Missy, on the other hand, was about two seconds from kicking him and his trouble-making brother out of her apartment.

"You are being completely unreasonable," Missy said through clenched teeth. "If you would calm down you would see that..."

"Calm." Brody let out a rough chuckle. "I am calm."

"You could have fooled me."

"Missy, answer me this." Walking in front of her, he ran his hands down her hair that was flowing free, and asked, "Did you wear your hair down for him? Did you let him stroke your hair? Fondle your breasts? Tongue that sweet pussy that belongs to me?"

"Nothing on me belongs to you," she thundered out, pissed off now beyond all belief.

"That's where you're wrong, princess." He dragged her close to him. "And if we're going to be doing any sharing of my property, then I'll be the one who decides who gets to taste you."

"Whoa," said Bryce, backing up.

Looking up in Brody's eyes, Missy said loudly and clearly, "There will be no sharing. No sharing, Brody."

"I don't know, Missy." He moved his hands down her back and cupped her ass. "You seemed to like the idea at the store."

Pushing herself out of his arms, Missy stepped away from him and eyed him and Bryce warily. "That was in the store, this is in my living room. This is not going to happen."

"And the difference is..." Brody said, moving towards her.

"The difference is, that was a fantasy and this is reality." Tilting her head to the side, she asked, "Do you really want to share me, Brody? Do you want to see some other man touching me?"

"Hell, no," he swore as he took her mouth with his. Missy was too angry to respond, but not angry enough to pound his head in with her cast iron frying pan. Pushing out of his arms, she breathed heavily as she tried to catch her breath. Brody was pissed off and aroused, if the bulge in his pants was any indication.

Bryce, who had been watching them like a ping-pong match, had made his way closer to the front door. "I think this is where I take my leave," he said to the couple, who weren't paying him any attention. "Remember, violence begets violence," he added and hurried out the door when they both turned and glared at him.

"You are being a dick, and tomorrow you're going to feel like an ass for behaving this way," Missy said, her frustration level rising like the hard-on held back behind his jeans.

"Are there any other body organs you'd like to call me before I start?" He walked towards her, forcing her backwards.

"Start what?" Her voice cracked under his stare.

"This," he replied, seconds before he dropped his mouth down on hers.

Running his hands all over her body, Brody ate at her mouth like a starving man. Pushing her back on the couch, Brody dropped between her legs and began to strip off her pants.

"Brody, let's talk about this," she said, trying to pull him back up.

"We'll talk later," he said, his voice thick with tension and need. "I have to get inside of you. Now."

"Turn off the light," she whispered, pulling her shirt above her head.

"Hell, no."

"Brody," Missy groaned, pulling her shirt over her front, shielding her body from his eyes.

"Goddamn it, Missy." He pulled away from her, fuming. His frustration radiated off him like steam from a bath. "Don't do this."

"Just the main light," she asked, looking at him hopefully.

"No."

"We can leave the light on in the hall," Missy offered weakly. She could tell by the look in his eyes that wasn't going to fly either.

"No," he ground out, groaning loud with his frustration. "I want to see you."

"You can see me with that light on."

"No, I want to see all of you. I want to be able to count every freckle, every mole..."

"Every stretch mark," she countered.

"I don't care about that shit."

"I do," Missy said, her nerves bunched up in her stomach. Brody moved away from her and stood with his back to her. Missy sighed and slipped her shirt back on. She had been right. This night completely sucked big, hairy balls.

Chapter Ten

Angry and frustrated, Brody still didn't understand this phobia Missy had about her body. He might have issues with possessiveness, but her issues with her body were going to drive him insane. He didn't know how many times he could fuck in the dark before he would become bitter with her for holding herself back.

And that was what it felt like to him. Like she was holding back a piece of herself from him. A very important piece he needed. It wasn't only that he wanted to see her, he needed to.

Brody felt Missy come stand behind him and his body tensed automatically. He was already holding on by a thin thread, and if she touched him, he didn't know what he would do.

"Don't," he said softly before she could touch him. He tried to steel his heart against her.

"What, now you're going to try to get mad at me?" she huffed. Missy walked around him until she was face-to-face with him and said angrily, "This all started because you came over here starting shit with Scott."

Lena Matthews

"And if I would have waited for an invitation, would you have left the lights on?"

"Damn it, Brody, you're not being fair."

"And you are?"

"Why can't you just let this go?"

"Because I won't let you put a limit on us." Brody saw the hurt in her eyes and hated he had been the one to put it there, but he was certain she wouldn't cave and he knew he couldn't.

"It's just this one thing."

"It will always be this one thing, Missy." His voice rose in anger, and Brody had to stop and count to ten to calm himself down. "Can you honestly tell me that a month from now, a year from now, you'll be more comfortable with being naked in front of me?"

"Maybe," she cried, her frustration level matching his. "But you're refusing to give me time to get used to this, to get used to us. It's only been a week. Less than that, if you count from the time we started fucking, then it's only been a day. I need time to shift, and settle with this."

"Give me a timetable, Missy," he demanded. She was making him feel unreasonable, and Brody thought that was insane. Was it unreasonable to want to see your woman, all of your woman, without straining your eyesight? "Let me know when you'll be comfortable with me being with you."

"I thought you said we'd go slow."

"And I thought you said I could have complete control?"

"You said the same thing."

"Well, then I say I want you naked now."

"Fuck that, it's my turn," she shouted, getting up in his face. "Remember me sucking your cock in the kitchen? Well that was your turn, and now this is mine."

Brody's cock instantly hardened as soon as she mentioned this morning. Missy wasn't one to talk dirty, and the sound of the word cock coming out of her mouth, mixed with the visual of this morning, had him hard and aching in seconds. And the thought of his passive princess trying to be in charge had his cock throbbing even more.

Missy was so not the dominant, he thought with an inner smile. Brody thought she might have bitten off more than she could chew in an effort to hide from him a little longer. It was funny and arousing all at the same time. Brody never was one to give up control. Hell, he didn't know if he could do it if he had to, but if Missy thought she could handle it, he would love to see her try. He'd give into her this once, but by God, it would be the last time.

"You want to be in charge, baby?" he asked huskily, his eyes narrowing with desire. Missy's checks flushed and for once he knew it wasn't from embarrassment. She was as turned on as he was, more so if that was possible.

"Yes," she said, shoving her finger in his chest. "My turn, damn it. I say the lights go off."

"What else do you want?"

"You in the bedroom, now." Turning on her heels, Missy stormed out the room, leaving an amused and aroused Brody to trail behind.

Following Missy, Brody shut the door and leaned against it as he watched her close the blinds. Her lips were pressed tightly together and Brody could tell that she was still angry at him for pushing her. Walking across the room, she dimmed the light next to him.

"Come with me," she said, walking to the bed.

Brody smiled and sauntered across the room, sitting down on the bed where she gestured. Sitting down made him even with her breasts, a view he would gladly look at any night of the week.

"What do you want me to do?" he asked. Brody's palms itched to be filled with her full bosom, to bury his head in them and love them until she screamed.

Missy frowned, as if trying to figure out what she wanted. "Take my shirt off," she finally said.

Brody hooked his hands in the hem of the shirt and slowly raised it so he could enjoy the view longer. Tossing the shirt on the ground, Brody lowered his hands and waited for his next instruction.

"I want you to get undressed."

"Can I stand or do I have to do it sitting here?"

"You can stand."

Brody moved around her and quickly undressed. Leaving on his teal silk boxers, Brody walked to her and sat back down.

"You didn't take those off," she said, pointing to his boxers, bulging with his erection.

"I didn't know you wanted me to."

"I told you to take off your clothes."

Standing up, Brody dropped his boxers and moved to sit back down, but was stopped by Missy's hands wrapping around his cock. She stroked him, forcing Brody to bite back a groan as his thick cock filled her hand. Looking up into his face, Missy wet her lips and said, "I know what I want you to do."

"What?" he said hoarsely.

"I want to watch you masturbate for me."

"Missy," he groaned as she tightened her hold on him, stroking him harder. "I thought this was supposed to be all about you."

"It is," Missy said, leaning forward and biting at his nipple. "And it will turn me on to see you do this."

"I don't know if I can do that," he admitted, closing his eyes in ecstasy.

"You can and you will." Releasing him, Missy quickly disrobed and climbed up on the bed. Throwing a sheet around herself, Missy plumped up the pillows behind her and waited.

Brody bit back a groan, this time one of irritation, not desire. She was hiding herself again. "I'm going to need something from you."

"What?" she inquired inquisitively.

"Missy, I need a little stimulation myself, sweetie." Brody gestured down to his cock, which although still hard, was not at full mast.

Making a gesture with her hand, she asked, "You mean you just can't..."

Smiling he said. "Sure, I can do that. I just need to see you doing things too, to help me along."

"Like what?"

"Why don't you touch yourself for me?"

"This sounds like you're trying to take over." She frowned. Her fist had tightened around the covers as if she was afraid he was going try to rip them out of her hands at any moment.

"No, sweetie, it's not." Walking around the foot of the bed, Brody stood next to her and started to stroke his cock slowly. "Just do anything. I won't force the issue. You can go as far as you want."

Missy nodded her head in agreement and lowered the sheet under her breasts slowly. Just the sight of her pale white breasts, with their large pink nipples resting next to the dark purple sheet, was enough to get his juices flowing again.

"I want to get on the bed next to you, baby."

"Okay."

Brody climbed up on the bed and moved next to her hips. Sitting back on his heels, he spread his legs slightly to give her a better view. The cool sheets felt soft and crisp against his bare flesh, and Brody tried to find the most comfortable position to get in so he could watch and be watched at the same time.

Taking his hard member in his hand, Brody stroked himself slowly, watching Missy watch him. He ran his hands over the head of his cock, spreading his natural lube.

Brody's eyes followed Missy's hands, slowly easing up the sheet, brushing against her breasts. Leaning back, she slid one hand teasingly over her nipple, rolling it gently between her finger and her thumb. Her nipple raised and beaded, allowing her to tug on it as she watched him with wanton eyes. Brody longed to lean forward and to take her nipple in his mouth, but he refrained, only going as far as she would let him.

Staring at her, he was so lost in the trance of her fingers, that he missed Missy calling him. When she called him again, Brody looked up from her hands and asked her to repeat the question.

"Do you need some lotion?"

"A little would be nice."

Releasing her breasts, she leaned over and opened her drawer, taking out a small tube of hand lotion. Sitting up, Missy squeezed the bottle, adding a drop of lotion to his purple head. Brody hissed as the cold lotion hit his hot flesh, but he soon worked it into his skin, warming it up as he stroked himself.

Missy dropped the bottle back in the drawer and leaned back, leaving the sheet bundled at her thighs, exposing the soft swell of her stomach but stopping inches away from what he really wanted to see. Brody bit back a curse when he realized that she wasn't going to show him more. Instead, Missy slipped her hands beneath the sheet and moved her legs open a bit.

Brody had to grip his cock harder as he watched the sheet move back and forth as she rubbed herself underneath it. He couldn't see what she was doing, but he had a general idea, enough of an idea to cause him to speed up his rhythm.

"Move the sheet," he said softly, looking up at her.

Missy obeyed without comment and spread her legs slightly. It was enough of a view he was able to see up to her lips. She caressed her breasts again before slowly opening her thighs and slipping her fingers between her legs.

Brody's head began to swim as he watched Missy pleasure herself in front of him. Never in a million years would he have thought she would have the nerve to do this, but here she was; lovely, spread open, and his. His mouth watered to follow her fingers, sliding against her swollen clit, and his cock ached to slip in between her twin folds and plunge itself to release.

He could hear the soft wet sounds of her pleasuring herself as he sped up his hand to match the rhythm of her thrusting fingers. He jerked hard on his length as the sounds of her pleasure filled his head. Brody fought to hold onto his control as her sweet aroma filled the air, urging him to taste her.

Missy switched hands and coated her hard nipple with the juices stained on her fingers, and Brody could not resist slipping forward and taking the wet nub into his mouth. Groaning, he tongued her nipple as he jerked his cock, tasting her musky flavor on it.

Releasing her nipple, Brody had to move back or else he was going to come before he was ready. He wanted to enjoy the sight of her fucking herself, knowing that she might not ever do it again. Missy took her abandoned nipple back in her hand.

A moan slipped past her lips as she sped up her hand. Arching her back, she tightened her hand around her nipple and groaned louder as she bucked her hips up, fucking her hand. Brody didn't think it was possible but Missy became even more beautiful as she pleasured herself before him. Her head was thrown back in ecstasy as she fought to hold her eyes open, watching him stroke himself.

"That's it, baby," Brody moaned, his eyes narrowing as his hand sped up. He shook with the need to come, but still he held back. He didn't want to come until she did. He wanted to watch her go over the edge before he lost control and came all over her. "Fuck that juicy pussy for me."

His words must have trigged something inside of her, because Missy threw back her head and screamed out his name as she came, humping her hand.

Seeing that sent Brody scrabbling up closer to her. Moving near her breasts, he sat up on his knees and pushed his cock against her damp nipple, rubbing the head back and forth as he steadily stroked himself.

The touch of her puckered bud, the sight of her arching back, and the feel of his hand sent his shaft shooting. His balls tightened and a rush of blood filled his head as a rush of pleasure surged through him. Brody stroked his cock and watched through half-opened eyes as his seed poured over her nipple down into the valley of her breasts.

Missy sat up and took his cock into her mouth, forcing a hiss from his mouth as she swallowed what was left of his semen from his cock. Brody continued to pump, releasing all of his cum into her waiting mouth as Missy rubbed the strands that had sprayed her over her breasts into her skin, using it as lube against her hardened nipples.

Her loving tongue caressed his sensitive head, so sensitive that despite the pleasure, he had to pull out of her warm mouth. Missy replaced his cock with her cum-coated fingers and licked them while watching him beneath hooded eyes. Reaching back into the drawer of her table, Missy took out a towel and wiped her moist chest before handing it to him.

Dropping back on his heels, Brody took the towel and cleaned himself before settling down next to her. Sitting with his back against the wall, he pulled her to him and placed her head over his pounding heart. Missy tugged on the sheets until he moved so she could cover herself again, and then lay against him, breathing in deeply.

Brody could not believe what he had just done, what she had just done. It was the most erotic thing he had ever done, the most erotic thing he had ever seen, with the most erotic woman he had ever known. What she lacked in courage, she made up with spunk. She was hot, sexy and more importantly, she was his.

"In a word," he teased, "*wow.*"

Giggling, Missy leaned into him more and looked up at him. "So do I get to be in charge more often?"

"Hell, woman, give me twenty minutes and a tall glass of water and you can be the boss again."

"So you liked it?"

"If I liked it any more I'd be in a coma."

"I liked it too."

"Really?" Brody leaned his head against hers and said, "'Cause I couldn't tell."

"Ass," Missy said, lightly hitting him in his stomach.

"Maybe next time."

"See, it's not so hard letting go sometimes."

"That's what I've been trying to tell you," he said, rubbing her arm when she stiffened up. "Settle down, princess, let me finish."

Missy grumbled, but moved back into him.

"You might be right and I could be rushing you just a bit."

"A bit," she replied sarcastically.

"Yeah, I said a bit, but I can't help my need for you any more than you can help your need to hide. So, I'll try to be a bit more patient, if you try to be a bit more comfortable with me. You know, a little freer."

"Freer than this?" Missy teased, running her hand down his sweat-coated chest.

Raising his brow mockingly, he asked, "You can be freer than this?"

"I don't know; let me be in charge more often and we'll see."

"Hell, baby, you've got a deal."

Chapter Eleven

Knocking on Kayla's door two days later, Missy waited apprehensively for her to open it, worried about how Kayla was going to react to the news Scott hadn't completed the survey. She tried calling him this morning, but his roommate said he wasn't in. Missy wasn't sure if he was really not in or just avoiding her. She hoped for the sake of their three-year friendship he was just not there.

Dylan, Kayla's fiancé, opened the door and smiled welcomingly at her. "Missy, come to deliver your *Walnut Weekly*?" he teased as he held the door open for her.

Missy smiled and walked in, used to Dylan teasing her about Kayla's project. Kayla, in her opinion, had definitely found a winner with Dylan. Not only good-looking and smart, Dylan had to be one of the nicest men she had ever met. He was always pleasant to her, smiling and joking whenever she came over. Dylan managed to do what few men had ever done in such a short time, make her feel completely comfortable around him.

His hazel eyes twinkled as he shouted over his shoulder, "Kayla, your Anal Accomplice is here."

"Damn it, Dylan, stop calling her that," Kayla yelled from the back of the apartment.

Winking at Missy, Dylan shut the door and said loudly, "Is Prostate Partner better?"

Missy smiled and laughed as Kayla muttered something incomprehensible before slamming out of her office, the guest bedroom of the apartment. Stomping out, Kayla looked fit to be tied.

Dressed in a purple shirt and green cut-off shorts, she stomped over to Dylan and kicked him in his shin with her neon-orange socks. "Ouch, Professor," he grimaced, rubbing his knee. "What was that for?"

"Stop insulting my help."

"I didn't insult her." He grinned. "She thought it was funny."

"I doubt it," Kayla huffed, irritated. "She was probably just being polite."

"Sorry, baby." Kissing her on the cheek, Dylan pulled her in close and nuzzled her neck. "I was just teasing."

"Keep that in mind when I reprogram the phone today."

"No, please, not that."

Pulling away from Dylan, Kayla smiled and winked at Missy. "That'll keep him in line." Taking Missy's hand, Kayla dragged her over to the couch and ordered over her shoulder, "Fix us a couple of drinks, please."

"Yes, your majesty."

Rolling her eyes, Kayla replied dryly, "I said please, sheesh."

Sitting down, Missy reluctantly handed Kayla the empty survey, biting her bottom lip in nervousness. Missy wasn't one for confrontation, and she didn't want Kayla to get mad at her. Kayla was one of the few women Missy genuinely liked, and she didn't want to disappoint her.

Kayla looked down at it and up again quickly when she noticed it was empty. "What happened?" she questioned frantically. "Didn't it work? Was it too large? What?"

"No," Missy reassured her, sensing her friend's worry. "No, it was all my fault."

Scrunching her brow, Kayla asked, "What do you mean?"

Missy filled Kayla in on everything that happened two days before, and to her relief not only was Kayla not mad, she found the whole thing hilarious. Dylan, too, and of course he couldn't wait to point out how The Walnut Wand was responsible for it all.

"That's not true," Kayla denied, throwing a pillow at him. "It's all Missy's fault for being utterly desirable."

Snorting, Missy said sarcastically, "Yeah, that's what it is."

"It is," Kayla pouted. "My poor little Wand was just caught up in the whirlwind of your torrid love affair, which I want more details on, and now I'll have to find a new subject to test it out."

Kayla looked over at Dylan with a speculative look on her face, causing him to pale and shake his head in denial. "Don't even think it."

"Honey, it's for science."

The ringing of the phone halted Dylan's reply, and by the way he jumped up to answer it, Missy thought he was happy it rang. Dylan held up a finger, to signal that he had to take the call, and walked quickly from the room. Kayla just smiled and shook her head. Leaning forward, Kayla whispered, "If I didn't know better, I'd swear that he just slipped his hand in his pocket and made his cell phone call home."

"Does he do that often?"

"Only when he wants to avoid a conversation." Kayla laughed. Setting her drink on the coffee table, Kayla tucked her legs underneath her and pulled her shirt down over her knees. "So, talk, woman, tell me about this trouble-causing man of yours."

"You kind of already met him."

"Who?" Kayla leaned forward excitedly.

"Remember the night that you and Eliza came to the shop?" Missy asked shyly.

"No!" Kayla squealed. "Not the hunk in the suit who passed you his card. You work fast."

"Not me, him. That man moves at the speed of light and doesn't know the meaning of taking things slow."

"Sounds to me like someone is in love."

"Not love," Missy denied. "But serious like, with a strong case of lust attached."

"Lust?" Wiggling her brows, Kayla grinned. "Does this mean that your books aren't the only thing you're cramming these days?"

"Kayla!" Shocked, Missy couldn't believe that Kayla had said that, although she shouldn't be surprised. Anyone crazy enough to invent an anal sex toy for men couldn't possibly have a shy bone in her body.

"What? Oh please, don't try that 'Miss Innocent' bull with me. I can tell he had more on his mind than the price of lube, and from the way you're grinning from ear to ear, I know he has to be doing something right."

"Oh, he does a lot right."

"Now that's what I'm talking about. Details please. Leave nothing to the imagination. Remember, I make sex toys for a living, so my mind is far too twisted to be left to come up with its own details."

"What do you want to know?"

"Let's skip all the boring stuff and get right to the goods. Is he?"

"Is he what?"

"Is he good?"

"No," Missy said, leaning forward. "He's great."

Kayla dropped her head back on the back of the couch and fanned herself comically. "I knew it. Something about a man in a tux."

"Well, he wasn't wearing a tux."

"I should hope not. So then, last night didn't cause any issues? You know, the whole Scott thing."

Missy sighed and shook her head. "Not really, but things aren't as good as I would like."

"Really? Why?"

"It's really a combination of things, but mainly he's a little, umm..." Missy paused, looking for the right word.

"Too controlling and overbearing."

"How did you know?"

"Honey, it's in the water in this town," Kayla teased. "But that shouldn't be a problem, he can change."

"My mother always told me that the only chance you get to change a man is when he's an infant in diapers."

"Ouch." Kayla grimaced. "Well, despite Dear Abby's words of advice, if he cares for you, then he will. It'll be hard and won't happen overnight, but it can happen."

Picking up her drink, Missy took a sip of her iced tea and held the cold glass in her hand. "It's not only him, although I wish I could pretend that it was."

"Then what else is it?"

"You only saw him for an instant and mainly from behind, but he's a very handsome man."

"And this is bad, why?"

"It's a little intimidating at times."

"Why?"

"Because he looks like that and I look like this."

Rolling her eyes, Kayla sat up and took the glass out of Missy's hand. "Look, there is a rule that I forgot to mention, and it's no self-deprecating remarks in my house. You leave that low-self-esteem bullshit outside on the curb."

"I don't have low self-esteem," Missy denied. "I have a mirror. I know what I look like and I'm fine with it. I love me for me. I just have a hard time accepting that he could too."

"And that's not low self-esteem?"

"No, I don't dis myself because of it."

"No, you just dis this man who cares for you."

"It's not like that."

"Then how is it?"

Growling, Missy picked up a pillow and buried her face in it. Looking back up, she said, "You are relentless."

"And you're annoying." Snatching the pillow from Missy's hand, Kayla threw it behind her and said, "He likes you because you're funny, beautiful, and a great person. Deal with it. No more whining or I'm going to have to knock you on your ass."

"You do realize that you were supposed to be cheering me up, right?" Missy said, crossing her arms over her chest. "On my side."

"I am on your side, and do you know what that says about me?"

"No, what?"

"That my side is the stupid side, and I don't want to be on the stupid side." Eyes widening as if she had a good idea, Kayla asked, "Can I change sides?"

"No." Missy swept the pillow off the floor and hit her with it. "You're on my side, damn it."

"Fine, but you have to smarten up, or I'm going to defect," Kayla grumbled.

"I just have to work up the courage, is all."

"To smarten up?"

"For a start, yes," Missy nodded. "But also to get undressed in front of him."

Kayla looked at her as if Missy had lost her mind. "You mean you've slept with this man and he's never seen you naked?"

"Well, not in bright light."

"Are you kidding?"

"No," Missy shrugged.

"And how does he feel about this?"

"How do you think he feels?"

"Well, you have to compromise."

"I am, we're leaving the light on, but it's dimmed."

"Have you tried lingerie?"

"That's not naked, Kayla."

"Apparently you haven't seen the right lingerie." Kayla smiled. "And I know just the place to go."

Missy looked over Kayla's colorful outfit with doubt. She didn't want to hurt her feelings, but she doubted that

Kayla's idea of sexy lingerie would coincide with Brody's. She could just imagine herself in a see-through orange negligee with a yellow bow tied in the back. Missy wouldn't have to worry about Brody being grossed out, he would be too busy laughing.

"I don't know if that's a good idea," Missy hedged.

"What's a good idea?" Dylan said coming from out of the back room. He had gotten dressed in a black suit and was fixing his tie as he came out. "Not another invention, is it?"

"No," Kayla said. "You have to go back to work?"

"Yes." Leaning down, he gave her a kiss and sat down on the arm of the couch. "Last minute hand-holding thing. So what's this idea?"

"I'm going to take Missy shopping."

"For what?"

"Clothes."

A huge grin spread across his face as he chuckled. "You're not picking out the outfit, are you?"

That was exactly what Missy wanted to know. Missy knew she wasn't the most stylish person in the world, but Kayla was ten times worse, plus apparently colorblind. But Missy was smart enough not to voice her concerns, unlike Dylan, who got a swat for his trouble.

"Look, buddy, I'm a genius. Right?" Kayla said frowning.

"That's what you keep telling me." Dylan smirked.

"Well, a real genius knows everything, including who to call in a time of fashion emergency."

"Who?" he asked, crossing his arms.

"Let's just say you guys are going to be one secretary short today. We're taking Eliza to lunch."

Missy couldn't remember the last time she'd had so much fun shopping in her life. Despite the fact that her credit card was burning a hole in her wallet, and she would have to work extra shifts to pay off her bill, which was now equivalent to the national debt, she was happy.

They not only went shopping for sexy lingerie, they also bought her some new, well-deserved outfits to finally update her sad wardrobe. Eliza not only knew the best place to shop, she also knew the best type of clothes that would suit Missy's full-figured body. Missy now had new pants and blouses perfectly tailored for her size.

Out were the big T-shirts that hung off her like oversized trash bags. Eliza had explained to her that because her chest was large it acted like a shelf, holding her shirts away from the rest of her body, forcing her shirts to jut out and fall straight down. It made her waist seem larger than it was, but now with her new shirts that were cut low, drawing attention to her cleavage and tightened underneath her breasts, the new fit of it made her waist seem smaller.

Eliza picked out slimming colors like blacks, grays and dark blues for her pants, and deep reds and purples for her shirts, to draw attention up to her face. Kayla had wanted her to get a few brighter things, but Eliza had vetoed that really quick and sent Kayla off to pick out under things.

The bras and panties Kayla had picked out were actually quite nice. Missy had been surprised and pleased. Kayla and Eliza both picked out a few sexy nighties and Missy couldn't wait to go home and try them on. Brody was going to flip.

After shopping, they stopped at a local deli to grab a bite to eat. Taking their sandwiches to a booth, they sat down and talked more than they ate. Missy had very few girlfriends in school, and it was a nice change to talk girl talk and to actually have a guy to brag about for once.

Sitting back, Missy looked at Kayla and Eliza and smiled. "Thanks a lot for today, you guys. I had a blast. I kind of felt like *Pretty Woman,* without the whore part."

Kayla spit out her soda, spraying the table, as she laughed hard. Chuckling, Eliza picked up a napkin and sarcastically wiped her face.

"Don't say stuff like that when I'm drinking," gasped Kayla as she wiped up the soda off the wooden table.

"Sorry. How was I supposed to know you didn't swallow?" Missy laughed.

"From the way I was sucking the straw, brat."

"No, really I want to thank you guys. I had a great time," Missy commented, looking at the two smiling women.

"Shopping is never a chore," Eliza said. "Unless you're dragging along a five-year-old."

"I know it took longer than we planned."

"I'm sleeping with the boss, I get side benefits. And if that doesn't work, I'm sure the sexy lace teddy I picked up will smooth everything out," Eliza replied, laughing.

"Dylan isn't a big lingerie guy." Kayla said, shrugging.

"That's because all of yours glow in the dark," Eliza teased.

"It makes it easier for him to find me," Kayla joked. "But seriously, Missy, do you think you're ready to blow his mind?"

"In these outfits, I better not have to blow anything." Missy winked, causing them all to burst out laughing again.

Chapter Twelve

Brody strolled through campus deep in thought. It had been two days since he saw Missy, and he didn't like it one bit. She'd had to work on Sunday, and he'd had a full course load on Monday; hopefully today they would be able to squeeze in some "us" time between classes and her job.

When he had talked to her yesterday, she had seemed really excited about getting together, but with one thing and another, it just hadn't happened. A lot had happened last night, though. He smiled as he thought back to how their simple goodnight phone call had turned into a bawdy, no-holds-barred phone fuck, but he wasn't sixteen anymore. He was tired of jerking off, especially when he had a hot, willing woman only minutes away.

Tonight he planned to pick her up from work and ply her with food, liquor and loving, and not necessarily in that order. Brody was going to triple-bolt his door, unplug his phone, and have the lights dimmed so she would have absolutely nothing to complain about.

After their talk on Saturday, he had made a conscious effort to refrain from mentioning the light at all. It still bugged him to no end, but he was going to try his damnedest to give her a little space and let her get used to him in her own time. Giving her time was probably the hardest thing he had ever done.

Brody had known from the first moment that he saw her, she was the one. Missy was the only person not catching on to that little fact. Brody had absolutely no intention of backing off, but backing down was something different. He wanted her to be as completely happy in their relationship as he was, or at least as he would be when she got over her little light phobia.

It was annoying, but everyone had their little peccadilloes. It wasn't as if she wanted him to spank her ass and call her Fred, although that could have its good points as well. Brody just had to learn to deal with her, because he refused to learn how to deal without her.

Brody strolled through the courtyard past the fountain and spotted Scott talking to a brunette girl with her back to him. Brody knew that Missy wanted him to apologize to Scott, and it was an idea that he was tossing around his head, despite the bile that rose in his throat when he thought about saying sorry to the prick. It was still up in the air whether he would do it or not. It just depended on his mood at the time.

Walking closer, he smiled when he saw Scott and the girl hug. *Good,* he thought, *now the bastard can get his own girl and leave mine alone.* As he neared the couple, they turned to sit, which caused Brody to stumble and almost drop over in shock. That wasn't just any girl. That was his girl. Only she wasn't wearing her normal clothes, she was dressed to kill.

Missy's curly brown hair had been highlighted, adding traces of blonde streaks throughout her full mane of hair. Instead of being up in its usual clip, her hair cascaded down her back, held back from her face with tiny butterfly clips. Instead of blue jeans and T-shirt, she was wearing black slacks with a V-cut, red baby-doll blouse. The blouse had short sleeves and was fitted tightly beneath her breasts, bringing her slim sides into view.

She looked amazing, and happy. And Brody, for once, was speechless. Looking up, Missy spotted him staring at her like a dolt and hopped up from the bench and hugged him tight.

"Sorry," she said embarrassedly as she moved to pull away from him. "I forgot where we were."

"Screw that," Brody wrapped his arms around her waist and pulled her in for a deep, soulful kiss. Pushing back, he looked down into her smiling face and asked, "Who are you, and where did you hide Missy?"

Laughing softly, Missy hit him teasingly in his chest. "I take it you like?"

Brody stepped back and surveyed her from head to toe again, and nodded his head. "Oh yeah, I definitely like."

Brody held her back and twisted his index finger around, gesturing for her to spin for him. Rolling her eyes, Missy twirled, giving him the full view. She giggled as she did it and Brody wasn't sure what made him happier. The fact she went shopping for new clothes or the fact she enjoyed them.

Walking back to him, Missy leaned forward and whispered in his ear, "I think you should apologize to Scott for the misunderstanding on Saturday."

"Not going to happen," Brody said firmly. He didn't want to hurt her feelings, but Scott kissing her was way over the line.

"If you do, I'll show you what else I bought. It's black and lacy and I'm wearing it as we speak."

"I can't apologize with you in my way," Brody said, moving Missy from in front of him. Brody walked purposefully to Scott, who visually tensed at his approach. Chuckling to himself, Brody immediately felt better. He knew without a doubt no matter what happened, Scott would now know Brody had a claim.

Scott stood when Brody was in front of him and nervously looked around, shuffling his backpack higher on his shoulder. Brody thrust out his hand and was rewarded when Scott jumped. Eyeing him, Brody knew he wasn't any competition, now or ever. He was a big pussy, and Brody knew how to handle pussies.

Brody waited for Scott to take his hand, his amusement skyrocketing as he felt Scott's sweaty palm in his. Squeezing harder than necessary, Brody got in one last physical jab, hoping Missy wouldn't notice. "Sorry about the other day."

"No problem, man," Scott said hoarsely, trying to ease out of the grip.

Brody's grin widened as he tightened his grip for a second longer before releasing Scott's hand. "My temper got the best of me, and it's not like I can fault you for your taste." Turning back to Missy, he winked and held out his hand.

Missy walked up to them and took Brody's hand. Smiling at Scott, she leaned her head against Brody's arm, which lessened some of his irritation over her smiling at Scott. Brody knew it was childish, but still, he wanted all her smiles. He always knew he was possessive, but he wasn't sure when exactly he had lost his mind and turned into jealous-stalker guy.

"Do you have time for a cup of coffee?" he asked, looking down at her.

"Sure. Let me get my stuff."

Brody let go of her hand long enough for her to get her things and then took it again as they walked across the campus. Ignoring the strange looks he was getting from people, Brody walked proudly with her hand clasped in his. Sure, she had been his student last semester, but this was a new semester. She wasn't his student anymore, so he didn't think he would get much shit. And if anything was said, he would just mention, none too politely, a few things he knew some of his fellow co-workers did. Brody wasn't above blackmailing to get his way.

Shutting the door behind them when they entered his office, Brody quickly dropped his bag and pulled Missy into his arms. They kissed as if it had been months instead of days since they had last seen each other. Her mouth opened under his and his tongue plunged into her mouth as quickly as his hand slid under her shirt.

The rough lace of her bra scratched against his palm, exciting him as he felt what she had teased him about outside. Her nipples hardened under his touch, catching up to the bulge forming in his pants. Moving back, Brody tried to raise her shirt, but was stopped by Missy's hand pushing down on it.

"I forgot," he said, walking over to the light switch.

Missy laughed and shook her head. "No, it wasn't the light," she teased.

"Then why the 'no'?"

"We're in your office, Brody."

"I know, but you promised me some goods, woman. Now deliver," he said, chasing her across the room.

Laughing, Missy walked backwards until she was pressed up against his waist-high bookshelf. Jarring the photos and awards on top of the wooden bookshelf, Missy stopped her retreat. Putting her hands behind her to brace herself, her breasts thrust high out in front of her, making his mouth water all the more.

"Don't tell me I shook his hand for nothing." Brody watched her like a tiger stalking his prey. Following her to the bookcase, he leaned forward and placed one hand on each side of her, caging her in his embrace. "'Cause I'm not afraid of going back out there and pummeling him."

"On school campus?"

"I'll run his ass off the grounds first. Remember, princess, I know thousands of ways to hurt a man without leaving a mark."

"More of that GI Joe shit, huh?" Missy teased.

"That's right, baby. I'm part of the few, the proud..."

"The cocky."

"You didn't have a problem with my cock the other night."

Missy leaned forward and cupped his cock in her hand. "I don't have a problem with it now."

"What, a few new clothes and you grow some balls?"

"Feels like you're the only one with balls here, baby," she whispered, tilting her head to the side and licking her lips.

"And that's how far I want to be inside of you right now—balls-deep." Bringing his mouth down to kiss her, Brody pulled back as he heard his office door creak open.

"Professor Kincaid," a female voice said from the cracked door.

Cursing, Brody pushed back, frustrated and pissed off. Stalking to the door, he jerked it open, shielding Missy from the view of the student. "Can I help you?" he angrily asked.

"I...I...wanted to talk to you about last week's assignment," she stuttered, stepping back from the door.

"My office hours are from one until three," he sneered at the brunette. He didn't know her name; it was something with a C or a T. Hell, they all were, but he knew that she didn't have an appointment. "Come back then."

"But it's twelve-fifty," she stammered, looking down at her watch.

"Which means it's still not one." Slamming the door, he turned away, not giving her another thought. He had more important things on his mind, and from the look on Missy's face, he was the only one.

"That wasn't nice." She frowned.

"I never said I was nice," he said, walking back across the room to her. "And if she's here to talk about an assignment then I have a ten-inch dick."

Widening her eyes, Missy joked, "You mean you don't?"

"As far as you're concerned, I do." Putting his arms around her waist, he tried to pull her in closer, but was stopped by her hands pushing against his chest.

"Brody, it could have been important."

"I have my hours set for an important reason."

"Quickies before class?"

"I'll make it worth your while," Brody wheedled, trying to capture her mouth with his.

"I won't be able to come with her out there," Missy said, moving her face to the side.

"Let me worry about that." Kissing her exposed neck, Brody nibbled up her ear before taking her lobe between his teeth and biting down softly. "I promise you it won't be a problem."

"No," she moaned, tightening her nails in his chest. Brody could tell he could make her give in, but he didn't want her to do anything she wasn't comfortable with.

"I want to see you tonight," he said, licking the inside of her ear. Brody felt her body shudder against his and had to bite back the urge to shove her against the wall and fuck her hard and fast.

"I have to work tonight," she said, caressing him with her hands. "But I get off at eleven."

"I'll stop by after my last class," Brody replied, kissing up her jaw. "What time do you go in?"

"Three," Missy whispered against his lips, softly kissing him.

"Are you going home now?" he asked, pulling back.

"No, I don't get out of class until two-thirty."

"Did you bring a change of clothes?"

"No," she laughed. "I'm wearing this."

"The hell you are," he fumed.

"What's wrong with it?" she asked, looking down at her outfit. "You liked it just fine a few minutes ago."

"I still like it, but I don't want you wearing that to work."

"Why?'

"Because it's too..." He paused, looking for the right word.

"Too what?" Missy frowned.

"Too revealing."

"Don't start, Brody."

"I'm not trying to start, but come on, Missy, your breasts are practically popping out of that blouse."

"They are not," she said, covering them with her hand.

"Yes, they are."

"Why are you okay with me wearing it to school and not to work?"

"Because at work you're surrounded by a bunch of horny perverts and at school..."

"I'm not?" she asked, smiling. Dropping her hands off her chest, she laughed as she shook her head in amusement. "You've been in the trenches too long, soldier boy. High school boys and college boys are the definition of horny perverts."

"I'm not kidding."

Sighing, Missy rolled her eyes and cupped his face with her hands. "I'm not kidding either, Brody. I'm going to work and I'm wearing this. So deal."

Jerking his head back, Brody had to fight back the controlling demon inside of him. "I don't like it."

"You don't have to," she said, dropping a kiss on his lips.

Taken aback, Brody realized that she was right. Missy was going to do exactly what she wanted and there wasn't shit he could do about it. Or was there?

"I'll see you tonight," Missy said as she picked up her discarded backpack from in front of his desk.

"Yeah." He shuffled around, thinking. If Missy thought she was going to have the last word, she was sadly mistaken. "I'll see you tonight."

With her hand on the doorknob, Missy turned back to him and said, "Shall I send in the next victim?"

"Funny," he grumbled, walking behind his desk. Sitting down, he tried to hide his still-erect cock underneath his desk and watched Missy swish out of his office. The old saying "what a difference a day makes" was no joke. His shy little princess was blooming right before his eyes, and he wasn't sure how he felt about it.

Chapter Thirteen

Looking cute didn't come easy. The lace of her bra was scratching her sensitive breasts, and her thong had all but disappeared into her abundant rear. It was going to take a crowbar to pry that sucker out of her butt, Missy thought as she tried to discreetly shift so that the thin string would slide out of its hiding place. She now knew for a fact that despite all the malarkey Eliza had slung, not every butt could survive in this deadly floss.

Other than the chafing she was sure she was experiencing, the purchase of her new clothes had been a good idea. Even Brody seemed to like them, after his initial shock had worn off. The look on his face was worth the itchy boobs, the lost floss and all the lewd glances she had gotten tonight. Although Missy would never admit it to him, he had been right about wearing this outfit to work.

Not that anyone had been rude or discourteous to her, but she had gotten a few too many glances at her breasts instead of her face tonight. Even Nick, her co-worker, had given her a double glance when she walked in tonight. Missy no longer doubted how good she looked; it was just probably for the best she didn't look this good at work again.

Putting down her magazine, Missy picked up the phone and went to dial Brody's number when the doorbell dinged, signaling that someone had come in. Putting the phone back in the receiver, she turned to the doorway and smiled when she saw Bryce strolling into the store.

In grease-stained jeans and faded blue T-shirt, Bryce looked handsome but dirty. He had a grease smear above his right brow, and his hands, although clean, seemed to be permanently stained brown.

Smiling, she walked around the counter and said, "Hey, Bryce, what are you doing here?"

"What, I can't pop into an adult bookstore on my way home from work for the sheer pleasure of it?"

"I have a hard time believing you need to come to a place like this for pleasure."

"I'm a lonely, lonely man." He winked at her. "Besides, I have a secret crush on a hot babe that works here. What do you think my chances are?"

"If you're talking about Patty, you're out of luck, she only dates women."

"Damn it, just my luck," Bryce said, snapping his fingers, pretending to be disappointed "And wouldn't you know it, I happen to like that in a woman. Oh well then, I guess it's for the best I had my eye on someone else. I was talking about this hot little brunette with legs that won't stop."

"You flirt."

"Is it working?"

"I think one Kincaid in a lifetime is enough, don't you?"

"It's the wrong one, baby."

"That's what all the Kincaids say."

Laughing, he leaned against the counter and looked around the store. It was only six, so the crowd was still kind of light. Tuesdays were good movie rental nights so Missy was expecting to get busy later near the end of the night.

"So, did you come to take advantage of our rent one, get the second one free offer?" she teased.

Bryce's eyes, so similar in shape and color to Brody's gray ones, twinkled and crinkled in the corners. "No, I just came to check out the scenery."

Something about that just didn't seem right, Missy thought as she narrowed her eyes, asking, "What are you doing here, really, Bryce?"

Saluting her, he replied, "Just following orders, ma'am."

"Whose orders?"

"Sergeant Brody Kincaid's, ma'am."

"Brody told you to come keep an eye on me?" Missy demanded, shocked.

A lazy grin spread across Bryce's face. Missy could tell he found the whole thing to be amusing; unfortunately, it was at her expense.

"Not an eye on you per se," he said amusedly. "More like an eye on that outfit, and may I add, *damn* you look good."

"No, you may not," she fumed. "I'm going to kill him."

"Well, you'll have to wait until eight, because that's when he's coming to relieve me."

"But his class isn't over until nine."

"I think he's closing up early."

"Arrg," Missy said, shaking her head. "Your brother..."

Nodding his head in commiseration, Bryce agreed. "I know. Mom has the same reaction."

"I'm going to kill him."

"You would be surprised how often I hear that phrase when it comes to him."

"And you think this is just funny?"

"As hell."

"You both are twisted."

"Once again, you're not saying anything that I didn't already know."

Stomping around the counter, Missy snatched up the phone and punched in Brody's cell number.

"He's in class now," Bryce reminded her, grinning like a fool.

"That's just fine," she muttered, waiting for his voicemail to kick on. His smooth voice came over the line, only enraging her further. He was so freaking controlling. That stupid, egotistical, con...

"Brody," she yelled into the phone after his voice message clicked off. "You're lucky this is a recording and not you because I'm so mad right now I could spit nails. You stupid jerk, who in the hell do..."

The phone clicked, ending her message, and that only pissed her off more. Slamming the phone down again, she turned and looked at Bryce, who was holding his sides, laughing.

"Shut up!" Missy demanded.

Bryce only laughed louder and harder. Missy picked up the Swiffer and hit him on the arm. He howled and jerked out of the way, still laughing, and Missy herself had to see the amusement of the situation. She was still pissed off at Brody, but it wasn't Bryce's fault, the damn fool. He was laughing like she was doing stand-up at the Apollo.

"It's not funny, Bryce." Missy walked back around the counter.

"It is a little," he said, holding his fingers marginally apart.

Sighing, she plopped down on her stool and shook her head in disgust.

"Cheer up, baby girl, it could be worse."

"How?"

"He could have asked some of his commando buddies to come over here in fatigues and case the joint."

Missy paled at the image. "He wouldn't?"

"He did that to my mother's last boyfriend." Bryce laughed.

"He's certifiable."

"That he is, but he's also crazy about you." Looking at her seriously, Bryce added, "So before you brand him with cooking ware, keep in mind his heart is in the right place even if his head isn't."

"I know," Missy said with frustration. "But it doesn't mean that it's not annoying."

"So make him pay tenfold tonight."

"Don't you worry, I plan to."

"Thatta girl." He grinned.

"You know you really don't have to stay."

"Sure I do. Brody asked me to do him a favor and I'm here. If the situation were reversed, he would do the same for me. It's a brother thing; you wouldn't understand."

Missy didn't get these two. They were almost complete opposites but closer than any two men she had ever met. Growing up an only child, she didn't understand the bond that came with having a sibling, and not for the first time, she regretted being alone.

Her mother and she had been close as only a single mother and an only child could have been, and when her mother died, she had felt like her entire world had died along with her. Missy had always wondered if she'd had a brother or a sister to share the burden with, if she might have turned out differently. Missy couldn't imagine Brody without Bryce or vice versa. They were lucky, and they probably didn't even know it.

The two hours passed quickly, especially since Bryce was such a joker. He teased and kidded her about everything. From customers to products, nothing was safe from his bawdy humor. He had even shared stories of his and Brody's childhood with her. Missy had laughed more tonight than she had in awhile, and she had to admit he made the hours go by quicker.

Twenty minutes after eight, Brody strolled in the door with his hand held behind his back. Missy was in the middle of laughing at one of Bryce's terrible jokes when she caught sight of Brody. She stopped laughing abruptly and frowned at him. Brody had the good sense to look sheepishly at her, because if he had come in all macho and commanding, Missy didn't know what she would have done to him.

Bryce turned and looked over his shoulder and smiled when he saw his brother. "Kept her warm for you," he teased, walking over to Brody.

Brody smiled slightly and slapped him on the shoulder. "Did you get much grief?"

"Not as much as you will."

"I was afraid of that," Brody said, looking over at Missy. Taking his hand from behind his back, he presented her with a dozen pink roses, her favorite. Missy's heart lifted a little because he had remembered what her favorite flowers were, but she wasn't going to let him get off that easily.

"Thank you." She gruffly took the bouquet into her hands. Lifting it, she inhaled the floral aroma and smiled into the flowers, careful to keep her face averted so he wouldn't see.

"Well, I know when my job is done," Bryce said, looking between the two.

"You don't have to go," Missy urged.

"No, I do have a life you know. A boring one, but a life nevertheless. And six o'clock comes earlier and earlier every day. I'll talk to you later, sweetie." Winking at her, he slugged Brody and said, "Call me tomorrow, bro."

"Will do, man. Thanks for coming down."

"No prob."

They both watched him walk out of the door. Brody turned to her when the door closed behind Bryce and asked, "So how much trouble am I in?"

"Tons."

"Got any weapons back there I should know about?"

"You're not funny."

"A little."

"No. Not at all." Missy laid the flowers on the counter behind her and turned back to him, frowning. "I can't believe you did that."

"I thought it was a fair compromise."

"A compromise!" she practically shouted. "Do you even know what that word means?"

"Sure I do. It means a settlement of a dispute in which two or more sides agree to accept less than they originally wanted. I'm an English professor, remember?"

"Way to go, Webster, but I don't recall you and I agreeing your brother was going to come baby-sit me."

"You need to be free to make your own decisions and I need to know you're safe. I think Bryce was a reasonable compromise."

"I didn't agree to it, Brody."

"And if I would have asked you, you would have said no."

"So you did it without asking me?"

"I'm trying, princess, I really am." Brody took her hand in his. "But you really have to meet me halfway. I know I'm a tad bit possessive."

"A tad?"

"Okay, maybe more than a tad, but I worry about you. This isn't the safest place in the world to work."

"The majority of the people who come here are just lonely, Brody."

"Lonely, horny people do crazy things all the time."

"This place is as safe as any other retail store."

"Maybe you shouldn't work retail."

"I like my job, and I'm not going to quit."

"I'm not asking you to. I'm just worried about you." Concern filled his eyes and his hands tightened around hers. "Just let me take care of you."

Sighing, Missy said softly, "There's a difference between taking care of me and smothering me."

"I'll move the pillow from above your face, if you cut me some leeway."

Laughing, she smiled. "You're a pain in my ass."

"Not yet, but the night's still young."

"Not for you, buddy, you're on punishment."

Leaning over the counter, he dropped a quick kiss on her lips and said, "I like the sound of that."

"I don't want Bryce coming here to keep an eye on me anymore."

"But what if he stops by to do some shopping?" Brody asked deviously.

Rolling her eyes, she looked at him, amused. "This isn't a grocery store, Brody. I might buy that once or twice, but if he's here every other day, I'm going to think your brother's got some strange habits."

"He does, trust me. I shared a room with him for fifteen years," Brody assured her.

"That's the same thing he said about you."

"Yeah, but he lies."

"And you don't?"

"Don't you trust me?" he asked coyly.

"With everything but the truth," Missy replied, laughing.

"Ouch."

"So what?" she said, coming from around the counter. "Do you plan to just hang out here until I get off?"

"Yep."

"And how long do you plan to do this?"

"Until you find another job, or I get arrested for stalking, whichever comes first," he said, grinning.

"You're twisted, you know?"

"It's been rumored, but is that how you talk to all of your customers?"

"You'd have to buy something in order to be considered a customer."

"I'm planning to."

Raising a brow, she asked, "What are you looking for?"

"I'm in the market for the perfect vibrator."

Missy stared at him, completely in shock. "What for?"

"Do you ask all your customers that?" Brody inquired, crossing his arms across his chest.

"Only the ones I'm sleeping with."

"Since it's for you, I guess I'll let you pick it out."

"I've worked here for three years and I've never bought one. What makes you think I'm going to buy one with you now?"

"Because I'm going to fulfill all your fantasies, remember?"

"And one of them was to get a vibrator?" Missy asked, confused.

"No, but I have plans for it," Brody said, wiggling his brows up and down. "Do you want to pick it out or shall I?"

"I think I should, just to be on the safe side," Missy replied apprehensively.

Walking with him down the aisle, Missy wondered what Brody had planned for her. None of her fantasies had included a vibrator and they had already masturbated in front of each other without the aid of any battery-operated devices, so she was at a loss as to why he wanted to get one.

Stopping in front of the hundreds of vibrators they had displayed on tables and racks, Missy looked at the pleasure sticks in a new light. She had stocked, ordered and even suggested a few for customers, but she had never looked at them with herself in mind. It all seemed strange now to her that they came in all shapes and colors. Sizes she could understand, but colors and shapes seemed a bit odd.

"Do you have a particular one that you want to try?" Brody asked from behind her.

"No, not really," she said, picking up the smallest one she saw. "We can take this one."

"Ah, no we can't." Taking it out of her hand, Brody slid it back on the prong and picked up a green one next to it. It was at least eleven inches long and shaped like a missile.

"Where do you think you're putting that?" Missy gaped at him as if he was crazy. There was no way anything that long and *green* was going inside of her vagina.

"Several places come to mind," Brody teased.

Snatching it out of his hand, she shoved it back on the prong and said, "No."

"What's wrong with it?"

"For one it's too big and for two it's green. Green, Brody. Nothing green is going inside of me."

"So I guess that leaves out cucumbers?"

"Gross." She shuddered, visualizing a vegetable sticking out of her hole. Missy could just imagine Bugs Bunny popping up in the corner of the room, and saying, "What's up, Doc?" Or worse, what if they didn't clean it properly and some pesticide got inside of her and gave her an infection. Scenario after scenario popped in her head, all grosser than the one before.

Picking up a purple one a few sizes smaller but of the same model, Missy held it up for Brody to see and offered, "This one."

Looking it over, Brody took it out of her hand and scanned it. Nodding his head, he replied, "Okay, this will do."

Missy had a customer waiting for her, so she helped him as Brody looked around some more. When the customer left, Brody strolled up to the counter and placed the vibrator, an egg, a butterfly and a remote control vibrator on the counter. Eyeing him warily, Missy rang it up and told him the total. Brody didn't even flinch at the hundred dollars plus total, he just handed her his card and signed the receipt.

Missy couldn't resist egging him a little more though. "You planning a party I should know about?"

"Are you worried?" he asked, taking the black bag in his hand.

"Should I be?"

"Trust me."

"My mother said never trust a man that says trust me."

"Your mother was a smart woman," Brody replied, winking. "I'm going to go throw this in the car, and then I'll be back."

"Is that a threat or a promise?"

"Both, baby, both."

Chapter Fourteen

Brody held the door open for Missy as she entered his dark house. Leaning over, he turned on the hall lamp, lighting the entryway. He was still surprised she had agreed not only to come over, but to spend the night as well. After she closed up they had gone back to her place and she packed an overnight bag and rode back with him to his house. Brody had big plans for tonight, and he didn't want her to leave so late.

And besides, they didn't get back to his house until after midnight, and the little bit of a gentleman that was left in him didn't want her driving on the street that late at night. Sure, it had more to do with him wanting her to sleep in his bed, but if she bought that excuse then he was a happy camper.

"Do you mind if I take a shower before we go to bed? I'm all itchy from the lace." Missy asked, walking to his bedroom.

Her mentioning lace was like a light going off in his head. They never did get around to her showing him her other purchases. "Sure," he said. "But do I get to see the thing you teased me with at work today?"

Smiling, Missy turned back to face him and said, "If you can be a good boy and look without touching, you can."

"Oh, I'll be good," Brody promised, walking towards her. "I'll be ever so good."

"Then come with me."

Brody took Missy's hand and walked with her into his darkened bedroom. Ignoring the light switch next to the door, Brody instead turned on the bathroom light and partially closed the door so that only a bare line of light was sifting through. Releasing her hand, Brody walked to his bed and sat on the edge, waiting for her to undress.

Missy put her overnight bag down by the bathroom door and turned to face him. Taking her glasses off, she set them on the entertainment center in front of his bed and walked back in front of him and stood in the direct line of the light streaming from the cracked door. Stepping out of her black mules, she unbuttoned her pants and slid them down her pale legs. Taking off her shirt, she stood in front of Brody in only her panties and her bra, both lace and sheer.

Brody had to take a calming breath when he saw her standing before him in all of her glorious beauty. The black contrasted against her skin like the stars against the black velvety sky. Her full breasts were held high and firm in the black web of her bra. Her dusky areolas peeked behind an intricate pattern of lace, and her nipples protruded like hard buttons on a blouse. The black panties lay high on her hips but were cut into a "V", seductively showing off her softly rounded belly and sexy navel. Brody wanted nothing more than to pull the underwear off with his teeth and feast on her.

"Are you going to put that back on when you get out of the shower?" he asked hopefully.

"No." Missy laughed. "It's dirty. I've been wearing it all day."

"I don't mind," he assured her.

"But I do. Don't worry, I brought something new to put on after I get out of the shower."

"If you look half as good in it as you do in this, I'm going to have a stroke."

"I'll put 911 on autodial then."

Nodding his head, Brody replied, "I'm going to need it."

Laughing, she turned, exposing her full globes to his hungry eyes. Her round cheeks were bare except for a T-shaped piece of fabric that lay between them. Brody moaned loudly as she swished out of the room, leaving him panting for more. He didn't know where she got this new flash of courage from, but he liked it.

Getting the bag of goodies out of the hall, Brody brought them into the kitchen and opened them. Carefully washing them with soap and warm water, Brody wanted to have them all ready in case they decided to use one or all of them tonight. Taking them into the bedroom on a kitchen towel, he laid them on his nightstand and inserted the video he had bought for them into the VCR.

Brody grabbed a pair of gray silk boxers, went to the guest bathroom, showered and shaved. Drying off, he put on the boxers, loving the feel of silk on his bare skin. Walking back into the bedroom, he came to an abrupt halt when he spotted Missy sitting on his bed, with the bedside lamp on, in a red sheer baby doll, rubbing lotion on her skin. Her long hair was still wet from the shower and lay in waves against her back.

Looking up, Missy smiled and set the lotion down on the bed. Getting up, she turned around, giving Brody the full effect of the red net shimmering around the top of her full thighs. She looked beautiful. Flushed from the shower, her skin was tinted pink and shone as rosy as the flowers he had given her earlier in the day. The top pushed her full breasts up until they damn near spilled out from their embroidered captor, and her pussy was hiding behind the sheer netting and covered by a triangle of red material held up by two twin strings nestled on her hips. Brody went from soft to hard in record time.

But he was torn. He didn't know if he wanted to rip off the gown and fuck her where she stood, or have her dance around him like the naughty little angel that she was. The baby doll covered her enough that he could tell she was comfortable being in the light in it, but it was all sheer enough he was happy the light was on. It enhanced her breasts and hid the flaws he knew she thought she had.

Rubbing his chin with the back of his hand, Brody asked hoarsely, "Is the drool apparent?"

Smiling shyly, Missy replied, "Money well spent?"

"Honey, I would give you the deed to my house to help pay for that outfit." Walking over to her, Brody reached out his hand and ran it over her bare, warm arms and down her sides, feeling the netting in his hand. Meeting her nervous eyes with his own lust-filled gaze, he said, "You look fucking amazing in this."

"Thank you."

"No, thank you." Leaning down, Brody ran his lips lightly against hers. He held back from her, because he had plans tonight that didn't include pounding into her as soon as he could.

Brody ran his hand down her damp hair and looked into her big beautiful brown eyes. His heart filled with emotions he had never felt before and words he had never uttered before stalled at his lips. He knew he was ready for love, but with Missy coming into her own, he didn't know if she was. Sighing, he pulled away and turned off the light she had flicked on.

Reaching into his nightstand, he pulled out his remote and turned on the TV. She walked to the entertainment center and put on her glasses before walking back to him. Pushing play on the VCR, Brody watched with amusement as she stilled, her attention on the video of a woman masturbating on a bed.

Climbing on the bed, Brody propped pillows behind him and pulled Missy down. Moving her between his legs, he held her back against his chest and his raging erection.

They watched the movie in silence for a while as the woman pleasured herself on the screen. A man came into the scene and Missy's breathing sped up as the actor pushed his cock into the actress's mouth. Brody slipped his hand inside the top of her baby doll and ran his fingers across her hardened nipples. He wasn't the only one who was enjoying the show, he thought with a smile.

Pulling her breasts out of the top, he rolled her pebbled twins between his fingers. "Pull your skirt up," he ordered, into her ear.

Missy complied without taking her eyes from the screen, even going as far as to press up on her heels, taking her bottom off the bed, so that she could take off her panties. Brody released one of her breasts almost reluctantly, reached over onto the nightstand and grabbed the egg. Handing it to her, he spread his legs, so that he could pull her back farther into him.

"Press the bulb against your clit," he instructed firmly.

She moved the egg-shaped vibrator between her thighs and jumped when Brody turned on the switch. Tilting her head to the side, he leaned forward and bit her gently on the neck as he alternated the speed on the egg. Missy's moans soon matched the actress's on the screen. Brody squeezed and teased her nipples, alternating between her two breasts as he sped up the egg.

"I love to watch you come," he whispered in her ear. "To know that you're coming for me, and no one else, drives me wild."

Missy shuddered and groaned as he teased her with the egg. Looking back at the TV, Brody saw another man join the first on screen and watched excitedly as he began to fuck the woman as she blew the other man.

"Do you like watching this?" he asked.

She was quiet for a moment before she softly answered, "Yes. Do you?"

"I'm a guy, so of course I like porn, but I'm enjoying watching it with you more. It's a complete turn-on for me." He squeezed her nipple and pushed his penis against her back, rubbing it against the silk and her. "I like watching you get aroused."

Moaning, Missy began to thrust lightly on the egg as he twisted her nipple. "Does it bother you that I'm aroused from watching this?" she panted.

Laughing softly, he asked, "Are you kidding? I love the fact that you're digging this. It turns me on to see them fuck, too."

"Have you ever done that?"

"No, and I don't have any real desire to," he said, biting her again. "I want to be the only dick in you."

"I want that, too," she groaned.

"But I'm willing to compromise."

"What...what do you mean?" she groaned, still pushing up on the egg.

"Lay down, baby," he turned the egg off, grinning when she groaned in disappointment. Pulling the egg up by the cord, Brody placed it back on the bed and grabbed the vibrator. Missy lay down width-wise on the bed, still watching the film. He smiled at his dirty little girl, fingering herself as she watched. Slapping her hand lightly, he said, "No, no, bad girl. That's my job."

She blushed and removed her hand, and then spread her legs invitingly. Brody took her glasses off her and placed them on the nightstand. Turning on the vibrator, he placed the tip against her clit and moved it in circles around her erect nub. She moaned and rocked her hips as he teased her with the purple toy. When he sensed she was nearing her climax, he moved it away and was rewarded with her groaning his name in despair.

"Patience, princess, I'll soon fill that hungry puss with something that will have you creaming even more." Taking the vibrator, Brody inserted it into her wet pussy, pressing it firmly in her tight hole. Arching her back, Missy pushed down on the vibrator and fucked herself with it as he held it firmly in his hand.

The sounds of her pussy sloshing down on the toy had him biting back a groan himself. She looked so fucking hot, all wet and horny, just as he wanted her to be. "Don't move," he ordered, pushing the vibrator in deeper, as he turned it off. Dropping his boxers, now moist a bit from his pre-cum, Brody climbed on the bed next to her face and reached down and turned the vibrator back on. Missy turned her head and opened her mouth, engulfing his hard cock into her hot mouth.

The movie played like a sex symphony in the background. Their own personal fuck music complete with moans, groans and shouts of ecstasy. Brody loved hearing the noise of the threesome on screen blend in with the moans that were coming from the back of Missy's throat as she sucked his cock. It was like a sonata made just for him.

He groaned as he fucked her mouth. Missy tongued his shaft as she worked his cock with her hand, and he had to concentrate so he didn't blow his load before he was ready. Moving to the side, he pushed the vibrator in and out, fucking her as she blew him. It was damn difficult, but the pain in his side was worth it because she was hunching up her hips, fucking the toy with all her might.

"Fuck it, baby, take it all," he urged as he watched her undulate on it.

Letting go of his cock, Missy groaned loudly as she came, flooding the toy and his bed with her juices. Brody pulled the vibrator out and flung it to the side. Moving down the bed, he buried his face in her pussy. Attacking her clitoris with his tongue, he feasted on her. Slipping his fingers in her wet hole, he fucked her as he ate her wet pussy.

Spreading her legs apart, he ran his tongue from the top of her clit to her rosette, slipping his tongue into her tight, forbidden hole. The sensation made her shoot off the bed, bucking as he licked her ass and fingered her hole.

"Brody, no, oh God," Missy chanted as she dug her fingers into his head, holding him forcefully in place. This was fine with him, because there was no place he'd rather be. Pushing his tongue in as far as he could, Brody moistened her rosette, preparing her for his finger. There was nothing he wanted more than to bury his cock in her ass, but he knew that it was something that he would have to work her up to.

Moving his mouth away, he drew his juice-covered finger from her wet pussy and slid it into her rosette carefully. Pushing in his index finger, Brody felt Missy's legs tighten around his head, trying to adjust to the new sensation.

"It's okay, baby," he whispered from between her thighs. "You can take it."

"Brody," she moaned. "I don't think I can."

"Just relax. I'm not going to fuck this sweet ass today." Moving his finger in and out slowly, he continued, "But one day I will. I can't wait until I'm buried all the way inside of you, fingering your clit as I fuck your ass."

"No." Tossing her head back and forth, she groaned as she pushed down on his hand, unknowingly allowing him to push further into her. "You're too big."

"You'll like it. No, you'll fucking love it." Brody paused to lick her clit before saying, "Come on, baby, just imagine my cock stretching your tight ass, your pussy weeping as I work my way in." She moaned and clasped her hard nipples in her hands, tweaking them as he told her of his plans.

"Then, when I'm finally in all the way, your ass will feel so full that you'll think you can't stand it. I'll start to pull out, only to push back in as I reach around and finger your clit before I shove my fingers in your pussy. Pumping your wet pussy with my fingers as I fuck you in the ass. You'll come all over my hand as I come deep in your ass."

Speeding up his rhythm, he took her clit in his mouth. Sucking it between his lips, he lavished her clit with his tongue and squeezed it with his lips, holding her down while she rocked against him, screaming as she came.

Adding another finger as she was writhing from her orgasm, Brody twisted it and rotated his fingers, spreading her ass as he drank in her sweet juices. His cock was straining from the need to come. Hard and aching, he fought back the desire to replace his pumping fingers with his throbbing cock. He wanted to possess all of her. Claim every one of her holes as his. So there would be no doubt in her mind or his, who she really belonged to.

Sliding his fingers carefully from her ass, he moved his mouth reluctantly from her. Kissing up her panting body, Brody moved her hands to the side and latched on to her nipple, tonguing it with the same furious attention he had shown her clit. Cupping her other breast, he squeezed and kneaded her puckered bud, alternating between the two.

Brody released her nipple and leaned over her. "Do you forgive me for making Bryce come to your store?"

Opening her passion-filled eyes, Missy licked her parched lips and said huskily. "Just because you made me come? No." Bringing her hands to the top of his head, she pushed down on it and said, "But eat me again, and I might change my mind."

Chuckling, Brody moved back down her body and did as she requested. Drinking in her sweet juices, he licked her to two more powerful orgasms before reaching over into his nightstand and pulling out a condom. Sliding it on, he slipped his cock into her hot, moist channel. Despite her wetness and his fingering, Missy was still tight, and he had to slow his thrusts down until she was able to stretch to receive him.

Brody propped himself up on his elbow as he slid all the way in, so he could stare into her whiskey-brown eyes. Looking deep into them, he saw what he thought was a reflection of his affection for her burning deep in her eyes.

"You're so fucking tight," he whispered again, pulling out a bit and pushing back in. "I love your pussy. The way it squeezes me so tight. It's like fucking a fist. It's so tight."

"God, Brody," Missy moaned, raising her knees up, angling her hips so he could slide farther in. "Fuck me, please fuck me."

Rising up, he did just that. Pumping in and out of her body, he moved like a freight train, forward and steady, giving her every inch, every ounce of his cock. Not holding back, he placed his hands on her waist and got up on his knees, so he could fuck her more steadily.

The movie forgotten, they did their own moves fit for the screen. He held onto her hips and thrust into her over and over again while she clamored under him. "Yes, yes, yes." Not able to hold back, Brody powered forward once more, spilling into her as she tightened around him, crying out her release.

The power of his orgasm made him tremble as he tried to withdraw from Missy's body. He felt that his legs and arms wouldn't be able to hold him and that his bones were a mass of quivering Jell-O. Pulling out, he rose on his shaky arms and plopped down next to her on the bed.

Their labored breathing was the only sound in the room that Brody heard as he struggled not only to gather himself together, but also to deal with the complex emotions coursing through his body. Never having been in love before, he didn't know if the tightening of his heart and the pounding in his head was orgasm-related or love-related. Whatever it was, he hurt and felt wonderful all at the same time.

Turning his head, he looked at Missy's delicate profile in the light and watched with pride as she raised her shaking hand up to push her damp hair off of her face. The depth of their loving never ceased to amaze him, it just seemed to keep getting better and better every time they made love.

Chapter Fifteen

Love wasn't supposed to happen this quickly or feel this strong so early in a relationship. Missy was confused and unsure about a lot of things but one. She was head over heels in love with Brody. They had spent so much time together in the last couple of weeks she had a hard time distinguishing his place from hers. Slowly but surely, more and more of her things had begun to find their way over to his place. It was getting to the point where she had to air out her apartment to get rid of the stale smell.

Brody's idea of a solution was for her to just move in with him, but she wasn't quite ready for that step. Although she slept over at his place five nights out of seven, she still needed the security of her own apartment as a back-up plan. It had become a point of contention between them, and he was no longer hiding his irritation about it.

They moved past several of her barriers. Everyone on campus was aware they were seeing each other and if Brody ever got any shit about it, Missy was unaware of it. She had been to family dinners, had hung out with Bryce and his flavor of the month as Brody like to call Bryce's ever-rotating crop of girlfriends, and Brody had even gone with her to Kayla and Dylan's wedding.

For once being a bridesmaid didn't make her feel so bad. Not only was she in a stunning full-length ice-blue dress that thankfully Eliza had picked out, she also had one of the hottest men at the wedding as her date. She had originally been shy about asking him to go with her because she knew most guys didn't like to attend things like that. But Brody jumped at the chance, he was actually one of the handful of men—okay, the only man—she had ever met who owned his own tuxedo.

And damn did he know how to wear it. His body filled it out in ways that James Bond never did. The suit was custom-made to fit his exact measurements. It accented his broad shoulders and long frame. In a word, he looked scrumptious. Even Kayla's Great-aunt Beatrice, who had to be close to a hundred, had stopped and stared. Brody was breathtaking and he was hers.

The wedding was held at dusk, in a gazebo trimmed with flowers and twinkling lights. It was a crowded, yet imitate affair, with only Eliza and her as the bridesmaids, and Chris and Paul, another friend of Dylan's, as the groomsmen. Kayla looked lovely in an off-the-shoulder ivory gown and for once she wasn't clashing. They had written their own vows, and there wasn't a female with dry eyes left after Dylan swore to conduct himself in her absence as he did in her presence.

It was a truly touching event and during the exchanging of the vows, Missy couldn't help but look over at Brody. His eyes were on her as well, and they stared at each other until the minister pronounced Dylan and Kayla man and wife. Walking down the aisle behind the happy couple, Missy smiled brightly and winked at Brody as she passed him.

The reception took place at a nearby Italian bistro, owned by one of Dylan's clients. The restaurant had an outside deck that was off the lake, and it too was decorated in lights and flowers, matching the gazebo where they had exchanged vows. They had hired a live band and everyone danced under lanterns embossed with Dylan's and Kayla's initials.

A cool breeze brushed over Missy as Brody held her close and they danced together under the stars and lantern lights. The romantic lyrics of Sade played softly in the background as he twirled her around the floor. This was what she had always imagined her wedding would be like. She would be in the arms of the man she loved more than anything in the world, surrounded by her family and friends. The only thing that was off was that she was in the blue bridesmaid dress instead of the ivory wedding gown.

"If I haven't said this to you yet today," Brody whispered in her ear, "let me rectify that right now by saying you look beautiful."

Pulling her head back so that she could look up at him, Missy smiled and said, "Thank you, and I too would like to add that you look mouthwatering. All the ladies are staring at your ass."

"They can stare all they want," he teased. "As long as they stare from a distance. Especially Kayla's great-aunt. She's giving me the willies."

"Aunt Beatrice is deadly," Missy teased back, looking around his arm at the purple-haired woman in a matching purple dress, who was watching Brody like a hawk. "If I were you, I would stay far from her and the kitchen."

"Why the kitchen?" he asked, warily looking over at Beatrice.

"Because she mentioned doing something with you and jam that the good Lord never intended."

Brody blanched at the comment and swished Missy in the opposite direction, heading away from the salivating senior citizen. Throwing her head back, Missy laughed happily as he spun her off the dance floor.

"Walk with me," he said, taking her hand and leading her towards the pier.

"Okay." Missy smiled as they passed people coming up from the lake and tried to take in every moment as if it was her last. If anyone would have told her months ago that she would be this happy, she would have thought they were lying. No way in a million years did she think it was possible, let alone normal, to be this happy.

"I have a present for you," Brody said, leaning back against the pier's banister.

Looking up at him smiling, Missy asked excitedly. "What?"

"A little something I saw that made me think of you right away."

"Nachos?" she teased.

Brody frowned, pulling his hand out of his pocket.

"Just kidding, sheesh," she replied.

"You may not get it now."

"Ahh, come on. I was just joshing." She wrapped her hands around his lapels, tugged him forward and brushed his lips with a kiss. "If you give it to me, I'll be ever so grateful."

Raising one brow, he asked, "How grateful?"

"Very grateful," Missy whispered, and she kissed him again, this time lingering long enough to swipe her tongue between his lips.

"Okay," he said when she pulled back. Reaching in his pants pocket, he pulled out a rectangular velvet box and handed it to her.

Excitement coursed through her as she took the heavy box in her hands and pulled it open slowly. Inside, nestled on the black velvet, was a bracelet blending fiery opals and icy diamonds, strung together with gold. It was the most beautiful bracelet Missy had ever seen in her entire life. The opals were brilliant in color, with slashes of blue and red entwined within the milky stones.

Gasping in shock, Missy gently touched it with her fingertips before looking at Brody who was grinning broadly. "Wow."

Laughing now, he unhooked it from its clasp and pulled it out of the box. Placing it around her wrist, he hooked it together, caressing her softly with his fingers at the same time. The paleness of her skin and the richness of the bracelet looked good together, as if one was made for the other.

Missy was stunned. Never in her life had she been given something so beautiful. With tears brimming in her eyes, she looked up at him, still speechless.

"Do you like it?" he asked hopefully.

Holding her arm out to the side so she could stare at it more, she replied shakily, "Are you crazy? Of course I do. But Brody, I can't accept this. It must have cost..."

"You can and you will," he said stubbornly. Tilting up her chin, he looked down at her and wiped away the tears that had escaped from her eyes. "And who cares what it cost? If I can't spend money on the woman I love, then who can I spend it on?"

Missy almost swallowed her tongue. Brody had never mentioned love the entire three months they had been together, and of course, when he did, the jerk did it surrounded by a hundred people. She wanted to jump on him and squeeze him to death, and bean him on the head at the same time. Missy felt overwhelmed and humbled. She knew she loved him, but she wasn't sure if she was comfortable just blurting it out there like that.

Brody watched her expectantly and when she didn't say anything his eyes narrowed a bit and he pulled back.

"Brody...I ..."

"It's okay, Missy," he said, with a smile that didn't quite reach his gray eyes. "I didn't say that expecting you to say it back. I said it because that's the way I feel."

"I feel the same," Missy said shakily. "I care for you so much..."

"Missy," Eliza said, coming up from behind them. "I've been looking for you everywhere."

Smiling at them, Eliza grabbed her arm and said excitedly, "Come on, girl, we have some more pictures to take."

"Oh, okay, I'll be right there," Missy said, still looking at Brody.

Smiling, he bent down and kissed her on the forehead. "It's okay, princess, there's time. Why don't you go smile for the camera, and I'll meet you by the bar when you're done."

Nervously, Missy fought the tug of Eliza on her arm, wanting to stay and talk with Brody some more. She was torn between her bridesmaid duty to Kayla and the hurt in Brody's eyes. "Are you sure?" she asked apprehensively.

"Yeah, go ahead, baby."

"We're only taking a couple of pictures, Missy, not going to war." Winking at Brody, Eliza said, "Why don't you go ask Aunt B to dance? It might do her old heart some good."

"Uhh no," he said laughing. "I think I'll go see a man about a horse instead."

They all walked back towards the party together, with Brody breaking away as they neared the family gathering for photos.

"If I wasn't already in love, I might have to perk up the twins and go after that man," Eliza teased.

"Your daughter is too young to be motherless," Missy kidded back. They both laughed as they positioned themselves around Kayla.

Although Missy smiled, her heart wasn't really in it. She was afraid that she might have damaged things between Brody and herself. The bracelet lay as heavy against her wrist as her heart lay in her chest. She just wanted to hurry up with the photos and go soothe things over between them.

Before the last flash had even faded from her eyes, Missy was walking towards the bar looking for him. It took a moment for her eyes to adjust to the darkly lit room, but she soon spotted Brody leaning against the bar. Brody had his back turned towards her as she moved past people to get nearer to him. As she stopped at his side she noticed a woman's hand lying against his and he was just moving out of the way when Missy walked in front of him.

She expected a look of embarrassment to come across his face, but was only met with a look of indifference.

"Am I interrupting?" she asked coolly. A lot cooler than she felt, that was for sure.

Brody looked at her a little taken aback, before his eyes filled with fire. "What do you think?" he asked heatedly.

"Why don't you tell me?"

"It looks like you've already made up your mind." Brody shoved away from the bar and towered over her. "No need for me to chime in here, is there?"

Missy looked from him to the stunning blonde dressed in a little black scrap of nothing lounging in the next chair and didn't know what to think. On one hand she knew Brody cared for her, hell he had just told her he loved her not a good ten minutes before. But they did just sort of have an argument, and in the back of her mind, Missy thought he could have been trying to get back at her for not saying "I love you" back. It was a game her ex, Tony, had played a lot. All the confidence she had built up in the last few months tumbled like dominoes. Her old doubts and insecurities hurtled back at record speed, and she was left wondering.

Brody just turned and walked away. Missy held back from following him and just walked away broken-heartedly as he pushed past people and stormed out of the door.

A nudge at her arm made her turn and she looked down into the wrinkled, cloudy-blue eyes of Kayla's aunt.

"You're not going to let him go, are you?" she croaked, nodding towards the swinging empty doors.

"If he wants to leave, who am I to stop him?" Missy asked, more to herself than to the older woman.

"You're a fool," she said, emphasizing her comment by banging her cane on the wooden floor. "If he was flirting with that floozy—" The blonde gasped at Beatrice's comment.

Beatrice narrowed her gaze, which made her eyes disappear entirely in a sea of skin and shook her cane at the woman. "That's right, I said floozy. Then you take him home and give him a lesson in manners, but you don't let him go home alone. You fight, then you make up."

Missy looked down at Beatrice with tears in her eyes and nodded her head in agreement. If Brody had been flirting with the blonde, then she was going to make him pay, but there was no way he was leaving without her. Running past startled guests, she pushed open the door and flew out into the night.

Brody had neared his car and was standing next to it with his hand on the roof, breathing heavily when Missy collided into him.

"What the hell?" he said, pushing away from the car. Turning, he righted them both and pushed her away. "What do you want, Missy? Want to make sure that there's no bimbo in the backseat for me to take home?"

"Well, what was I supposed to think, Brody?"

"That I was having a drink."

"She was touching you," Missy yelled.

"But I wasn't touching her," he yelled back. "Did you happen to notice me pushing her hand away?"

"Yes, but…"

"But nothing," he thundered. "Do you really think I would tell you I love you in one moment then go flirt with some bimbo minutes later? What kind of person do you think I am?"

Missy fought back the shame that was coursing through her. "I'm not going to feel terrible about this, Brody," she said, poking her finger in his chest. "You get jealous all the time."

Taking her finger, Brody pushed it away from his chest like it was merely a fly. "And it's always because I don't trust other people around you, not because I don't trust you," he replied softly.

The softness of his voice and the hurt in his eyes caused Missy's heart to skip a beat. Deep inside Missy knew, despite his calmness, Brody was dead serious and extremely hurt. She didn't want to cause a scene, and she refused to lower herself to beg him to stay, but she was truly at a loss as to what to do.

"It's nice of you to make that distinction now when it's not you who was acting jealous."

"Can you honestly say that you ever felt like I didn't trust you?"

"That time with Scott," she hedged.

"If it was you I didn't trust, why was it his balls I had pinned against the wall?"

"Why are you turning this around?" Missy cried.

"Because I'm tired of always being the one out there alone on the edge."

Feeling confused, Missy stepped back and stared at him. The sounds of cars going by and the party still going on inside were the only noise in the calm, cool night. Brody's chest rose and fell sharply and his face was aflame in anger that matched the heat in his stormy gray eyes.

"You're not the only one," she replied quietly.

"Bullshit!" he spat angrily.

"It's not bullshit, Brody."

"Yes, it is. I'm the only one giving here." Counting off on his hand, he continued, "You don't want the lights on, the lights stay off. You refuse to look for another job, although you know it kills me worrying about you at that place. You won't consider moving in with me. Hell, you can't even tell me you love me. It's all me giving, all me changing, all me willing to give a fucking inch."

Missy wanted to deny it, any of it, but she knew she couldn't. Brody had made countless overtures, always giving while she sat back on the sideline waiting for the other shoe to drop. With a look of defeat etched onto his face, Brody turned back to his car.

"I'm sorry," Missy said, wanting with every fiber of her body to beg him not to go.

"I know, Missy," Brody replied, without turning around. "You're always sorry, but this time I can honestly say I don't care."

Brody unlocked the driver's door. Opening it slowly, he asked, "Can you find another ride home?"

"Yes," she said sadly.

Nodding his head, Brody got in the car and shut the door behind him. Missy stepped away from the car and watched in silence as he backed up and drove away. Missy stayed in that exact position staring after him. She cried, watching him leave until she could no longer see his tail lights, until she could no longer see the distant glimmer of his car, until she no longer had tears left to cry.

Chapter Sixteen

Tequila and bad country music were poor ways to mend a broken heart. The tequila made Brody sick, and the music just made him depressed, and, well, kind of sick too, he thought, turning the channel on his radio. It had been three days since his blowout with Missy and nothing had made him feel better yet, not even knowing he was right for once, and not just being a stubborn ass.

Well, not being a *huge* stubborn ass, anyway. Part of him could understand her getting jealous when the woman was coming on to him, heaven knows he got pissed off when another man even looked at her, but damn it, she should have had more faith in him than that. He had just told her he loved her for Christ's sake, and those weren't words he used lightly, or ever, outside his family.

To think he had even bought a ring and had made plans of proposing that night, he had to be a damn fool. It was obvious she wasn't in love with him, although he'd thought she was. Apparently he'd been wrong.

Pacing back and forth in front of his couch, Brody had to force himself not to call her or drive to her apartment. He was afraid of what he might do or say. On one hand he wanted to shake some sense into her until her head rattled, but on the other he wanted to throw her to the bed and ravish her until she admitted she couldn't live without him, the way he knew he couldn't live without her.

The ringing of the phone brought him out of his self-imposed funk. Storming across the room, he snatched up the phone and bellowed into the line, "What?"

"Still haven't made up with Missy, I see," Bryce said sarcastically.

"Does it sound like it?"

"You two need to sit down and talk this out."

"Who asked you, Dear Abby?" Brody growled, continuing his futile pacing. By the end of the night he was sure his calves would be killing him. He couldn't count how many times he had made this trip tonight, but he was sure he'd worn a patch in his taupe carpet.

"No one, dickhead. I'm trying to be supportive."

"By calling me a dickhead?"

"It's familial concern with a twist."

"What twist?"

"The kind where I care, but I'm not going to let you turn into a sissy la la. Snap out of it and go over to her house and work this out."

"I can't," Brody said with a sigh, sitting down on his couch. Leaning back, he closed his eyes and groaned softly.

"Why?"

"Because I need her to come to me."

"You're going to let your stupid pride..."

"It's not all pride, I swear, man." Opening his eyes, he rolled his head to the side and looked over on his fireplace mantel at the small, black velvet box sitting like a beacon in the night. "I need to know that she cares enough to give."

"Are you asking her to give more than she can?"

"I hope not, because I need this, Bryce. I need to be as important to her as she is to me."

"I know she loves you, man," Bryce replied softly.

"I wish I could be that sure."

"How about I come over and we play some cards, watch bad cable porn and tell lies."

Chuckling softly, Brody replied, "You don't have to, I'll be fine."

"I want to, besides I could use some extra cash. I'm a struggling young entrepreneur."

"Not that young."

"Fuck you."

"Nah, you have too much back hair."

"Ass," Bryce replied amusedly. "Give me an hour and I'll be there."

"Thanks, man."

"That's what brothers are for."

Brody hung up the phone feeling pounds lighter. His brother had always been his rock and his best friend, and if he had to get drunk and listen to shitty music, there was no one he would rather do it with. Turning the radio to the classic rock channel, Brody cranked up the volume to wash away the melancholy blues that had filled the air only minutes before his brother's phone call.

Pushing the couches out of the way, Brody set up his poker table, complete with chips and cards. Looking down at the felt table, Brody thought back to the last time he had used it, remembering the fun he'd had teaching Missy to play. Shaking his head, Brody refused to dwell on thoughts of her; he was going to have a good time if it killed him.

Brody headed to the kitchen to grab some snacks for him and Bryce when the doorbell rang. Looking down at his wristwatch, he shook his head. Bryce must be really worried about him, because he was forty-five minutes early.

"Lost your key?" he asked, pulling the door open. The smile dropped from his face as he came face-to-face with the woman who had been haunting his dreams and filling his every waking thought.

"I never had a key," she commented, looking at him curiously. Missy was dressed in her old clothes, baggy jeans and oversized black T-shirt, with her burgundy backpack swung over her left shoulder. Her trademark ponytail was back in place, along with the wary look in her hazel eyes.

"What do you want?" Brody asked coldly.

"To see you," she said, moving past him into the house. Walking into his living room, she paused at the table and looked over her shoulder at him, smiling. "This brings back memories."

"Did you come to walk down memory lane, or did you have a reason?"

Frowning, she set her backpack on the couch and faced him. "You make it awfully hard to apologize when you're being a jerk."

"Well, don't let me keep you," he said tightly. Brody could have kicked himself for saying that. He didn't want her to leave, but the way she showed up, so blasé, just irked him. Missy was acting like nothing happened, as if at most they'd had a little spat.

Facing him, she smiled warily and said, "Look, the way I acted Saturday was..."

"Childish, untrusting, bitchy..."

"I don't need your help filling in the blanks," she replied heatedly. Her cheeks flushed and she swiped her hands across her forehead, moving her bangs back. "I was wrong, but I can't believe we can't work this out."

"I don't know, Missy," he said stubbornly.

"Why not?" she asked with frustration. "Why are you making this so hard? I was wrong. I'm saying I'm wrong. I didn't make you eat shit after the incident at the apartment."

"This isn't just about you being jealous, this is about trust, and how you don't trust me."

"The bimbo had her hand on you."

"I'm not talking about trusting me with other women." Brody had to calm himself down. This was exactly why he didn't want to deal with her right now, he was afraid that he was going to erupt and Missy would be the one to suffer.

"Then what are you talking about?"

"I'm talking about trusting me with you. Your body, your heart, your life," he said harshly.

Missy took a step back and looked up at him with tear-filled eyes. "That's not true."

"Yes, it is," he bit out, walking towards her. "You don't trust me enough to let me in."

"You've been in plenty of times."

Brody stepped over to her and tapped her gently. "Inside your sweet pussy, but not inside your heart."

Missy captured his hand in hers and held it pressed against her chest and said tightly. "You are in my heart," she said firmly. "I didn't get to tell you on Saturday, because we were interrupted, but I do love you, Brody."

Brody stared at her in shock. He didn't expect her to say that and he was floored. His hand lingered for a moment against her soft breasts before he pulled it away slowly. "If you love me, how could you think that I would do that?"

"Because I learned the hard way love isn't always enough."

"I'm sorry, Missy, but that wasn't me, and I refuse to pay for someone else's mistakes."

"I know that it wasn't you."

"You must not."

"I do," she insisted. "It's just that if you've ever been hurt like that..."

"I was, Saturday."

"You will never know what it is like to be in this body."

"There's nothing wrong with your body." Brody was tired of her hiding behind her size. "I can tell you a thousand times, but until you believe it, we're always going to have this issue between us."

"You may think there's nothing wrong with it, but I don't live in Brodyland. I live in the real world. And in the real world I'm far from perfect."

"I..."

"Let me finish," she interrupted. "This isn't about you, this is about me. And you're right, this is my problem I have to work through, and I'm trying, but you have to be patient with me, 'cause I've been in this body for twenty-six years, you've only been in it for a few months."

Brody grunted, acknowledging that she was right, as she continued, "My problems are mine. If you want to be a part of my life, you're going to have to get used to me not feeling cover model-like sometimes, but I'm a work in progress and damn it, you're not perfect either."

"I never said I was."

"No, but sometimes you act like it." She fumed, "You're controlling, jealous and pigheaded, but I love you, all of you. And I'm taking the good with the bad, and if you want to be with me, you have to as well."

Looking at her mad and inflamed, Brody was amazed at how much she had changed since he'd first met her. He could remember first seeing her in class, shy and seemingly timid, and now she was vibrant and alive and demanding that he accept her for who she was. If he weren't already in love with her, he would have fallen head over heels right then and there.

"I do want to be with you," Brody said. "But it has to be all the way, Missy, or none of the way. I can't, I won't settle for half of you. I want the whole damn package. Every bossy inch of you."

"I'm not bossy."

"The hell you aren't. But I'm serious. I want nothing between us anymore. No more hiding in the dark or behind exes."

"I'm not going to be forced into this, Brody."

"I'm just letting you know where I stand."

"And where is that?"

"By your side if you let me." Taking her hand, Brody brought it to his chest and held it over his heart. "Trust me enough to love you, faults and all. Perfection is for women who are airbrushed, with staples in their stomachs. I want you, thick you, thin you, whatever size you come in. You're a work of art. Trust me enough to know that I know my heart and that it's yours."

"Love me for me."

"I already do," he said, dropping a kiss on her parted lips. Deepening the kiss, Brody released her hand and brought his to her waist. Taking her shirt in his hands, he tried to raise it but was stopped by Missy's hands on his wrist.

"Missy," he groaned against her mouth.

Pulling back, Missy smiled up at him, her eyes still bright with tears, but this time happy tears, he hoped. "Explain this to me, how do you go from angry to horny in less than a minute?"

"I'm a man, honey, I was horny the minute I opened the door." And it wasn't a complete lie. Brody always wanted her, whether he was pissed or not. She was like a slow, aching, fiery need in his body and soul, and he knew that she always would be.

"Good thing I wasn't the pizza delivery guy. That would have been one hell of a tip."

"I'll give you a tip, all right," he said rubbing his hard cock against her middle. "If you want to keep this shirt rip-free, I suggest you take it off right now."

"I want more than sex."

"It's always been more than sex between us, Missy."

"I love you, and I don't just want to make up tonight, if the problem is still going to be there tomorrow."

"I can't guarantee that we won't argue tomorrow, or the next day, but this is life, not heaven, we don't have to be perfect."

"Good thing for me," she joked.

"Don't do that," he said seriously. "I don't want you to say negative things about yourself. You belong to me." Holding up his hand to silence her, he continued, "Just as much as I belong to you, and I hate it when you do that."

"I'm just joking, Brody."

"Well, it isn't funny. It's demeaning to you and to me. If you hate your body so much, then do something about it."

"Wow, what a concept, I wonder why I never thought of that," she said sarcastically.

"Stop it."

"You know what, let's make a deal," Missy said, walking around him. Grabbing the cards off the table, she continued, "I'll play you for it."

"What?"

"If I win, you have to bite your tongue every time I say something you don't like."

"And if I win?" he asked, arching a brow. This whole night had done a complete one eighty. He had started it moping and a tad bitchy, with the only thing to look forward to belching and lying with Bryce. Now he had

Missy at his side again and he was about to get lucky. Life didn't get much better than that.

Missy gestured with her head over to the card table and said, "You want to see the goods, you got to earn them."

He knew that they had just simplified a shitload of problems and boiled them down to the bare necessities, but like Missy, they too were a work in progress. He was going to have to give her time to grow and she was going to have to give him time as well. "Gonna make me work for it, are you?"

"Yes, let's put your proverbial money where your mouth is. You want me to take it off, you better have a better hand."

"I taught you the game, don't you think I'll have an unfair advantage?"

"All's fair in love and war."

"Are we at war?"

"No."

"So for every hand I win, you take off an item and for every hand you win, I take off something."

She rolled her eyes at him. "That is how strip poker works."

"Seems like it's a win-win situation to me," he said, rubbing his chin, thinking.

"You have a problem with those odds?" she questioned, raising a brow.

"Not at all. I'm a betting man, the house always has the advantage, and since I'm the house, I'd be a fool to turn down them odds." Crossing his arms across his chest he continued, "Name your game."

"Five card stud, of course."

"Anything wild?"

"Jokers."

"I don't normally play with those," he noted, walking with her to the table.

"This isn't a normal game."

"So true." Sitting down across from her, he shuffled the cards. "Although I don't understand why I have to get naked if you're playing for me to shut up."

"Consider it a bonus for me, and a way to distract me for you," Missy commented, tapping her fingers against the table and watching the cards carefully as he shuffled them. If Brody didn't know better, he would think she didn't trust him, as if he would cheat. Well, he would cheat, of course, if he thought he could get away with it, but he doubted Missy would even give him the opportunity.

"No, I mean, do I still get to see you?" he asked as he dealt out the first hand.

"You didn't win, did you?" Missy picked up her hand and looked down at her cards. Rearranging them in her hand, she looked up at him expectantly.

Pausing, Brody looked over at her, not really paying attention to his hand. He should have known there would be a catch. Nothing was ever simple when it came to Missy. "So I could be playing all this for nothing."

"It's the luck of the draw," she shrugged.

"I told you luck is only ten percent."

"Then you better get to praying, because I don't plan to lose." Her eyes twinkled over her hand, and Brody knew that she wasn't bluffing. If he didn't win she wouldn't strip, and there was no way in hell he was going to miss her coming-out party.

Meeting her eyes, he replied huskily, "Neither do I, princess."

Chapter Seventeen

Missy played her hand like her very life depended on the outcome of the game. She still was apprehensive of being completely bare in front of Brody, but she wanted him to know she trusted him. And if she won and could put off the inevitable for just a few nights more, all the better. It was something Missy knew would happen eventually, but still she wanted to win.

Then there was the erotic factor of playing strip poker with your lover. Brody's body was exquisite and she couldn't wait for him to show it to her one piece at a time. They had started tonight with their relationship hanging in the balance, and now just a few minutes later they were facing off, playing for each other's clothes. Love was strange, Missy thought with a smile, and they were even stranger.

"I have three of a kind," she placed her cards on the table.

Brody grumbled and threw his cards down without even showing her what he had. Pulling his gray T-shirt over his head, he dropped it unceremoniously on the floor next to the table. Missy couldn't help but ogle his chest, perfect in all its glory, and wonder, for the millionth time, how she ever ended up with a man this fine. Of course, she thought it to herself, not even venturing to say it aloud, for fear of his response. She wasn't in the mood to get her ass paddled. Well, she thought with a small smile, she could be in the mood if he played his cards right.

"What, I don't get a little sexy dance?" she inquired teasingly.

"Only if you're willing to return the favor," he said, beginning to stand up.

"No, that's okay, then," Missy stopped him before he got all the way up. She didn't want to dance a little dance if she had to get naked. The thought of her body parts wiggling around wasn't appealing, so she might as well shut up.

Shuffling the cards, she asked casually, "So, were you going to call me if I didn't show up?"

"Eventually."

She snorted. "What's that mean?"

"That means once I was through pouting, I would have tracked you down and we would have hashed this out. You probably would have gotten mad and then we would make up and have hot, sweaty sex after you declared that I was right and I am the lord and master of all I survey."

"So you admit you were pouting?" Dealing the cards, Missy refused to acknowledge the rest of the shit coming out of his mouth. If it helped him sleep better at night to think that's how it would have happened, who was she to shatter his illusions?

"Is that the only thing you took from that?" Brody picked up his cards.

"I have selective hearing."

"What woman doesn't?" he snorted.

"How many do you want?"

"Give me two." He put down his two unwanted cards.

Missy's hand looked dismal at best. She didn't even have an ace, so she couldn't ask for four; instead she settled for keeping the two of spades and jack of hearts. Dealing herself three cards, Missy groaned when she saw that all she had was a measly pair of fours.

"What do you have?" she asked, holding her hand close to her face. The real crappy thing about this game, she thought dispiritedly, was that there was no bluffing when it came to the cards in your hand. Either you had the better hand or you didn't, and she knew from the smug smile on his face he had the better hand.

"A flush, what about you?"

"Nothing worth mentioning." She threw her hand down disgustedly. "Do shoes count as one item?"

"No, I was only wearing a shirt, jeans and underwear, so you get three things too."

"You didn't say that at the beginning."

"I'm saying it now. Shoes and socks don't count, and your bra and panties count as one."

"That's not fair." Missy wanted to whine, but she knew that she should have set the rules at the beginning of the game. She was playing against the man who taught her, what the hell had she been thinking?

"This is poker, it's not about fair. It's about how you play the game," Brody remarked, smiling as if he didn't have a care in the world, but he was the one sitting while she got naked, so maybe he didn't.

"It's only about how you play the game when you're winning," Missy said in frustration. Toeing the heel of her shoe, she slid it off and then did the same to the other foot. When her shoes were off, Missy took a deep breath and pulled her shirt over her head. *It's not a big deal*, she repeated to herself over and over again. *He's seen more of me than this, even if my fat is poking out of the side of my bra.*

Sucking in her stomach, Missy tapped her fingers nervously on the table, impatient for Brody to deal the next hand. Waiting for him to shuffle, Missy looked up and noticed that he wasn't even shuffling the cards.

Brody waited until she met his eyes before winking slowly and saying, "Those are the best pair I've seen all night."

Flushing, Missy groused, "Just deal the cards."

Missy had checked out books at the library and surfed the Internet looking for hints and suggestions to become a better poker player, and no matter how hard she studied, it still came down to the luck of the draw, and that completely sucked. She wanted to win so badly she could taste it, but with only two betting items left, she wasn't so sure of her chances. Maybe if he could bluff or fold, she might have stood a better chance of walking away from the table with her clothes fully intact, but at this rate, Brody only had to have two more good hands and she was screwed, both figuratively and literally.

"Your wish is my command," Brody teased, dealing out the next hand.

This hand was a lot better than her second one had been. She was already showing two pair, that alone was pretty good; if she lucked out and got a joker or either another five or another queen, she would be in seventh heaven.

"I'll take one," she said confidently.

"Ohhh, only one, huh?" Brody handed her a new card and said, "I think I'll take two."

The card was neither a five, queen nor a joker, but Missy still felt solid with the hand she held. "I've got two pairs."

Laying his hand down in front of him, Brody said, "And I've got three of a kind."

"You're cheating," she accused, looking down at his cards and back at his smirking face.

"Those are harsh accusations. There are penalties for accusing the house," he warned.

"Yeah, like what?" Missy didn't really think he had cheated, but anything to buy time seemed like a good idea.

"Like you must apologize on your knees with my cock in your mouth."

"Seems like it would be kind of hard for you to hear me if my mouth is full."

"I can read lips."

"Read this," she fumed and mouthed, "fuck you."

Brody roared with laughter and sat back in his chair, crossing his hands together on his flat abs. Missy looked down at the cards again, trying to gather the courage to stand up and drop her pants.

"What type of bulbs do you have in these lights?"

"Sixty, hundred, I'm not sure. Why?"

"Just seems awfully bright in here to me." Missy thought about her options, she could either stand up and drop her pants as quickly as possible and hope that he was blinded by her pale skin, or she could stay seated and perform a contortionist act and try to remove her pants without getting out of her chair. The only real problem was if she tried it that way, all of her fat would jiggle on top or worse, she'd fall out of the chair, landing in an undignified position Brody would take as a mating call.

Fuck it, she thought as she stood up and unbuttoned her pants. Looking at Brody, who was staring intently at her, she took a deep breath and dropped her pants, at the exact moment that Bryce walked in the room with a six-pack under his arm.

"Fuck," she said, grabbing at her pants and falling forward in the process.

"You and your timing." Brody laughed, getting out of his chair. Bending forward, he pulled Missy up, who was still struggling with her pants.

"I'm beginning to think it's impeccable," Bryce was snaking his head around, trying to get a glimpse of Missy.

"Oh my God. Oh my God. Oh my God." Missy chanted over and over again. This was worse than the time Bryce caught her giving Brody head. At least then she had been covered.

"I'm assuming this is a private game, although I'm willing to take off my shirt so I can catch up with you two," Bryce teased.

"Don't take this the wrong way, little brother, but get out."

"Leaving." He did an about face. Pausing at the door, Bryce said over his shoulder, "Love the panties."

Missy groaned again and buried her face in Brody's neck. Brody just chuckled and rubbed her back as she moaned in despair.

"If it makes you feel better, I'm more than sure he's nearsighted."

Missy snorted. "I don't believe you."

"I can punch him in the eye and he'll never look at another living thing again."

"I'm beginning to feel a little better." She giggled on his chest. Her life was an homage to Murphy's Law. Anything that could go wrong normally did. Pulling away from Brody, Missy buttoned her pants back up and walked to the couch. Grabbing a pillow, she encircled it with her arms and pulled it back against her like a shield. Any desire she might have felt walked out of the door the second Bryce did. If this was a prelude to their life together, they either had to get new locks or a bell for Bryce to wear.

"How pissed off would you be if I said I was no longer in the mood to play?"

Sighing, Brody walked over to her and dropped down on his knees in front of her. "Don't do this, Missy."

"I'm not, I'm just asking."

"I would feel pissed off, and I would go track Bryce and kick his no-knocking ass all over the street."

Laughing, Missy sat back and looked down at him, smiling. "That did kind of lessen the mood for me."

"Yeah," he said dryly. "Bryce has a way of doing that."

"I suppose you just want me to drop my pants and for us to pick up where we left off."

Rolling his eyes, he replied, "That would be the ideal situation, yes."

"I'm going to kill your brother," Missy said, gathering her nerve again. She had been doing fine before Bryce barged in, or as fine as she could be, seeing how she'd just dropped her pants. She would just have to buck up and try again.

"Not if I kill him first."

"Trust me." Getting up, she dropped the pillow back on the couch. "Me being naked isn't worth going to jail for."

"That's debatable," Brody murmured, getting off the ground.

Standing in front of him, Missy took a deep breath and reached for her button again. Looking into his hungry eyes, she paused. "Brody..."

"Do you remember the first paper you wrote for me?" he asked.

"It was on Shakespeare, I think."

"Yes, the assignment was to write what you think Shakespeare's take on romance was," he reminded her gently, pulling her hands away from her button.

"I remember." Missy wondered where he was going with this. She couldn't figure out what a paper and getting naked had in common, but she was willing to listen if he was willing to talk.

"To paraphrase your paper, you surmised that Will was a misogynistic unromantic man who probably had mother issues, and was more than likely gay," he smiled.

"I'm not a big fan of Shakespeare."

"I could tell by your paper," Brody laughed lightly. "But the thing that impressed me the most was the balls it took for you to say that. I had spent an hour raving about his work and you tore apart everything I said and pointed out that the true name of *Romeo and Juliet* was *The Most Excellent and Lamentable Tragedy of Romeo and*

Juliet. That they never stood a chance because of his take on love and women.

"You made me think and you aroused my mind way before you aroused my body. You're smart, beautiful and brave, and I admire you just as much as I love you. Don't back down now."

Unbuckling her pants, Brody looked her in the eyes as he pulled them open, not bothering to unzip them. Missy saw the desire in his eyes and gave in. Feeling secure in his love, she pushed her pants off her hips and let them fall to a puddle on the ground. Although she was secure, she still was a bit self-conscious and sucked in her stomach, hoping to downplay the bulge. Security only went so far.

Brody didn't even bother to look down, he just maintained eye contact and rubbed her arms gently with his hands, offering her comfort with his simple touch. "One more hand?"

"But you still have two items," Missy remarked.

"One hand, winner takes all," he whispered, brushing his lips against hers. The kiss was light and gentle, much like him, and it ended just as quickly as he had started it. Brody took her hand and walked her back to the table, pushing her chair in for her. As he passed the fireplace, Brody pocketed something she couldn't see before sitting in his chair.

"Do you want to shuffle?" he asked, holding the cards out to her.

Missy nodded and took the cards. Something felt strange, as if a lot was resting on this final hand. It was more than her clothes, it was more than his silence; it was more like their relationship was hanging in some kind of balance. Dealing the cards, she looked up at him, trying to read his expression. Brody's face was blank, and for the first time that night, Missy wasn't so sure she wanted to win.

Looking down at her hand, Missy was surprised to see she had dealt herself three aces. That was surprising and exhilarating, but instead of crowing, she kept silent and tried to school her features. Taking a calming breath, she slowly placed her other two cards down on the table and waited for Brody to make his wager.

"I'll take two," he said, staring into her eyes.

"I'll do the same," Missy replied, trying to sound calm. Brody only smirked and waited for her to deal.

With a shaky hand, Missy dealt out the cards before setting the deck down nervously. Closing her eyes for a moment, she said a silent prayer and picked up her cards, adding them blindly to her hand. Opening her eyes slowly, Missy almost shouted for joy as the joker smiled back at her.

"What do you have?" Brody closed his hand and laid them face down on the table.

"I dealt, you tell first," she said, a lot more calmly than she felt.

"A simple flush." He turned his hand over one card at a time. Missy held her breath. Her four of a kind would beat his flush if it weren't a straight or a royal. Brody flipped over a queen, a jack, a four, and a seven of diamonds and Missy let out a sigh of relief. It wasn't a straight or a royal. She had won.

Her feeling of victory lasted briefly as he flipped over the last card. It was only a two of clubs but sitting on top of it was a diamond ring.

Missy's eyes widened and she looked up at him, startled. Brody was watching her carefully, waiting for her reply. "It's a diamond," he said carefully. "The two carat kind."

"That's a hell of a hand." Missy was still in shock. Her cards trembled in her hand as she looked down at the ring and then back at him.

"I thought so." Brody let out a deep breath and asked, "So, do I win?"

"I don't think I can trump that." Missy laid her hand face down and fought the urge to reach across the table and grab up the ring like it was a lifeline.

"You looked pretty sure of your hand a few seconds ago."

"Yeah, but talk about having a wild card."

"Is that all you have to say?"

"Is there something else I should be saying?" Missy tore her gaze away from the ring and looked at him completely for the first time since he had turned the card over. For once Brody didn't seem so sure and cocky, he looked as jumbled as her insides felt, and it only made him all the more attractive to her. "It's not like you asked anything."

"If I did, what would you say?" he questioned, feeling her out.

"I guess we'll never know until you do," she said, smiling. Missy felt tears welling in her eyes, a glimmering shine that was equal to the one in Brody's eyes.

"I know that this isn't the most romantic way to do this, both of us half-dressed, sitting at a green felt table. But if you have the courage to do this, then so do I. Missy, I love you, and I want to spend the rest of my life with you. Will you marry me?"

"Can I think about it?" she joked. "But I want to wear the ring and tell everyone that we're getting married while I'm thinking on it."

"You can think as long as you want." Brody picked up the ring and walked around the table. He pulled her chair back, got down between her legs and took her left hand with his. Sliding the ring on her finger, he said, "Just as long as you know I'm not willing to make love to you again until you agree to marry me."

"I don't think you can hold out that long." Missy wrapped her arms around his neck and pulled him closer. Looking over his shoulder, she stared at the ring glimmering on her hand and smiled down at him. She was half-naked in the arms of the man she loved. Life didn't get much better than that.

"Do you want to make a bet?"

Epilogue

Missy wanted to kill Brody. He was mean. He was a beast. He was going to make her come before Kayla opened the door. Biting back a moan, Missy reached out and grabbed his arms as the butterfly vibrated against her clit. Brody only chuckled and held her upright. She fought back the urge to scream as she came for the second time since they left the house.

Not knowing when to stop had never been a real problem for Missy until they had gotten engaged. Now she'd found the daring side of herself and bet Brody to do almost anything. Hence, the dilemma she was faced with tonight. One simple warm-up hand, she had called it, a practice round before tonight's big game. And to make it more interesting she dared him to make a little wager. If he won, she would wear the toy of his choice to the game tonight, and if she won, he had to let her be in charge again for a night. Payback was a bitch, she thought as aftershocks rocked her body. She was going to get even if it killed her.

Missy didn't think he would really make her stick to the bet. Hell, she let him get away with making love to her before she said yes, although to be fair, he had made her scream "yes" several times before he fucked her that night, but still, she'd hoped he would reconsider. She should have known better; she was coming and he was amused. Life sucked.

Gathering herself together, she looked up into his laughing eyes and muttered, "I hate you," as she snatched her hand off him and stood seconds before Dylan opened the door.

"I didn't think you guys were going to make it," Dylan teased as he pushed the door open. "What happened?"

"Missy was coming..." Missy elbowed him in his ribs, earning a chuckle from him and a confused look from Dylan.

"Coming to a decision about what to wear," she finished lamely, her face flushing, giving away her lie.

If Dylan knew she was lying, he didn't say anything, unlike her pig of a fiancé.

"Did you forget whom I'm married to?" Dylan asked, smiling, shutting the door closed behind them. "There's no dress code."

"I heard that," Kayla muttered, walking up behind him and slapping him on his shoulder. Leaning forward, she gave Missy a warm hug, and than turned and did the same to Brody. "Ignore him, he's just trying to psyche me out for tonight. He knows I'm going to kick his ass."

"In your dreams, woman," Dylan pulled her to him and hugged her tight.

"What's with all this kissy-face stuff?" Chris walked out of the kitchen with a bag of chips in his hand. "We're here to play poker, not play the newlyweds game. See, this is why women shouldn't play poker."

"I heard that," Eliza said, walking from the back of the apartment. "And if I remember correctly, Kayla and I kicked butt last time we all played together."

"That's only because we let you win," Chris denied, sitting down at the table. Looking up at Dylan, he said, "Right, man?"

"Keep me out of this," Dylan said, holding up his hands.

"Whipped, man, see what happens when you get married?" he kidded, winking at Missy. "What do you think, Brody?"

"I think that there are a number of really great woman poker players in the world," Brody replied, sitting down at the table. Missy was proud of him. That was, until he finished with, "But lucky for us, none of them are at this game."

The men rolled with laughter and the women glared at them. Missy would have said something in their defense if it weren't for the butterfly turning back on. Glaring at a smirking Brody, she quickly dropped into a chair before her legs gave out on her. If he didn't stop messing with the remote, she was never going to be able to concentrate. "You okay, honey?" he questioned nonchalantly.

"Fine," Missy replied through clenched teeth.

Kayla sat down at the table and began to shuffle the deck. Handing the cards to her husband, she asked, "Do you really think you're a better player than I am?"

"I wouldn't say better," he hedged.

"What would you say?"

"I think women are more emotional when it comes to the game." Dylan shrugged his shoulders as Chris and Brody nodded their heads in agreement.

Gasping, Kayla looked around the table and said to Eliza and Missy, "Did you hear that bull?"

"I'm trying to ignore it." Eliza rolled her eyes. "You have to consider the source, we're talking about a bunch that keeps saying how bad we are but refuses to acknowledge that we've beat them."

"You only win because we let you," Chris replied cockily. "Right, Dylan?"

"Well..."

"Well what?" Kayla demanded.

"Whipped," Chris replied for him, laughing as Dylan flipped him off.

"You seem to forget that we're getting married in less than two months, dear," Eliza said picking up her cards. "Stop acting like an ass."

"Yes, dear," he replied, not even sounding contrite.

Brody and Dylan both looked at him and in unison said, "Whipped."

"I want you three to take it back," Kayla said, anteing up.

"Let it go." Dylan laughed. "If you're the better player, you'll prevail."

"But you'll say it's because you let me win."

"She has a point," Missy chimed in, then bit her lip as Brody slid his hand under the table and sped up the butterfly. "Stop it," she muttered, kicking at him under the table.

"Ouch!" Chris jumped.

"Sorry." Missy blushed. "Pass that to Brody for me."

Brody just chuckled as the group turned and stared at her. He was dead, she kept murmuring over and over in her head. If she survived tonight, she would kill him. After she fucked the shit out of him, of course, he was a dead man.

"Will do," Chris replied, laughing.

"I think we need to make a bet." Kayla set her cards down in front of her.

"Good God," Dylan uttered in disgust. "Again?"

"It's the principle." She crossed her arms over her chest.

"I agree," Eliza said, crossing her arms as well. "You guys don't respect our ability, and I know for a fact that we've beaten all of you."

"Even a broken clock is right twice a day." Brody smirked.

"Is that a bet?" Missy looked over at him. She was barely able to focus, but the little energy she wasn't using to fight the butterfly, she used to concentrate on the conversation at hand.

"You want to go twice in one night?" he teased, winking at her.

"If it means wiping that smug look off your face," she stammered, just as his hand slid back under the table. Missy closed her eyes and bit her lip as Brody turned up the butterfly full speed and she held on to the table as she fought the orgasm ripping through her body. "Oh God, Oh God," she muttered as she jerked forward and came, flooding her jeans with her essences.

"You feeling okay?" Eliza asked, leaning towards her.

"Fine," she ground out. Looking over at Brody, she mouthed, "I'm going to kill you," as he shut the butterfly off.

"I'm open for some bets."

"Me too," Chris grinned. Winking at Eliza, he continued, "I won big last time we did."

"I think we all have." Dylan smiled over at Kayla.

Missy looked around the group of friends and lovers and she knew that they all had walked away winners somewhere down the line. Not one of them could complain about the outcome of the game when they had all won big.

About the Author

Lena Matthews spends her days dreaming about handsome heroes and her nights with her own personal hero. Married to her college sweetheart, she is the proud mother of an extremely smart toddler, three evil dogs, and a mess of ants that she can't seem to get rid of.

When not writing, she can be found reading, watching movies, lifting up the cushions on the couch to look for batteries for the remote control and plotting different ways to bring Buffy back on the air.

You can contact Lena through her website: www.lenamatthews.com.

Look for these titles

Now Available

Call Me
Three Nights